THE NOTORIOUS
IZZY FINK

THE NOTORIOUS
IZZY FINK

Don Brown

A DEBORAH BRODIE BOOK
ROARING BROOK PRESS
NEW MILFORD, CONNECTICUT

Copyright © 2006 by Don Brown

A Deborah Brodie Book

Published by Roaring Brook Press

Roaring Brook Press is a division of Holtzbrinck Publishing Holdings Limited Partnership

143 West Street, New Milford, Connecticut 06776

Library of Congress Cataloging-in-Publication Data

Brown, Don, 1949-

The notorious Izzy Fink / Don Brown.— 1st ed.   p. cm.

"A Deborah Brodie Book."

Summary: In the 1890s, thirteen-year-old Sam copes with poverty and violence on the streets of New York's Lower East Side.

ISBN-13: 978-1-59643-139-3   ISBN-10: 1-59643-139-3

1. New York (N.Y.)—History—1865–1898—Juvenile fiction. [1. New York (N.Y.)—History—1865–1898—Fiction. 2. Poverty—Fiction.] I. Title.

PZ7.B81297No 2006   [Fic]—dc22   2005032970

Roaring Brook Press books are available for special promotions and premiums. For details, contact: Director of Special Markets, Holtzbrinck Publishers.

Book design by Jennifer Browne

Printed in the United States of America

First edition September 2006

2   4   6   8   10   9   7   5   3   1

ACKNOWLEDGMENTS

Although a novel might have one author, more than one mind—and heart—contributes to its creation. This is certainly true of *The Notorious Izzy Fink*. Everyone at Roaring Brook Press has showered Izzy and me with support, enthusiasm, and encouragement. Simon Boughton and Deborah Brodie make dreams come true for writers, or at least this writer, and I offer them my heartfelt thanks. And I am especially in Deborah's debt for showing an old dog many new tricks.

It's impossible to ignore the contribution of New York City's "newsies." Reading about their 1899 strike against William Randolph Hearst's *Journal* and Joseph Pulitzer's *World* newspapers inspired me to re-create their world in *The Notorious Izzy Fink*. News articles from competing and unstruck newspapers such as the *Times* and the *Tribune* offer a vivid and colorful window onto that era, and I borrowed from them shamelessly. Many of the stories are available on the Internet. Once inspired, I turned to other sources for information: *Jews Without Money*, by Michael Gold, and *Haunch, Paunch, and Jowl*, by Samuel Ornitz—both are memoirs of the Lower East Side and the turn of the century masquerading as novels. Also, Stephen Crane's novel *Maggie: A Girl of the Streets* and Herbert Asbury's nonfiction study of the city's underworld, *Gangs of New York*. Perhaps the book that best captures the flavor of the times is Luc Sante's nonfiction *Low Life*. (It's also great fun to read.)

Finally, gratitude to my wife, Deborah, and daughters, Sheahan and Corey, for putting up with a husband and dad who stares off into space more than most.

In memory of Ron Nadel

CONTENTS

FIGHTING FINK

I clocked Fink so hard on the side of his head I coulda sworn it rang like a bell. I can't say for sure because hitting that stone-hard skull of his stung my hand so bad that I couldn't think about nothing else.

I had spied Izzy Fink among the shoppers clogging Hester Street, him lifting apples from a pushcart while its owner was distracted by a customer. I stopped dead and tried to melt into the throng before Fink could see me, and would have succeeded, too, if it weren't for the apple salesman finally getting wise to Fink's felonious deeds and chasing him off, sending him crashing into me and leaving both of us reeling.

"Damn!" he barked as he bounced off me, then stared at me in disgust.

I expected to be swarmed by his gang, but nothing happened. He just stood there and gave the stink-eye to me. Fink's alone, I said to myself.

"Yer on the wrong street, Paddy," he said.

I smiled. Fink didn't have the nerve to shake me down

and take the eighteen cents I had in my front pants pocket. Him and me might both be thirteen, but I'm taller, though skinnier.

"Ya better watch out next time, ya Mick bastard, 'cause if I catch ya with my gang, you'll really get thumped!" he snarled.

Actually, what he said was more like, "Ya betta vatch out, ya Mick bastud, cuz if I catch ya wid my gung, ya vreally get tumped." Izzy is off the boat from Russia only a few years ago, and his words spill out of his mouth like a greenhorn's, all rough edges and splinters.

He glared at me for a moment, leaning forward on his short, thick legs while balling his meaty hands into fists.

It was seeing them fists that set me off. Maybe that idiot Fink might surprise-punch me, I thought. Not seeing the angle in taking seconds, I let him have it first.

Crack!

I wanted to hit him in the ear, somewhere soft, but Fink ducked at the last second and my knuckles landed at the band of his cap. My hand went numb, like it got smacked with a hammer. I blew on it and shook it, trying to get it back to life. Fink? He turned in circles, moaning, pressing both hands to the side of his head. If my hand hadn't hurt so much, I'd have hit him again in the snoot or knocked the cloth cap from his nut. He kept twirling and moaning until the crowds of Hester Street shoppers swallowed him up and he disappeared.

Geez, I thought, a fight with Fink wasn't the grandest way to start the day.

I had planned to sell newspapers with Manny Goldberg on Broadway, and had set out from home, the whole time keeping my eyes peeled for danger, like Fremont among the Red Men. Every street has its own gang, and life could be miserable for the kids from outside, getting shaken down or taking a beating or both. I thought I'd gotten by Hester Street scot-free. Meeting Fink was bad luck, him being the boss of the Hester Street gang and me being something of an interloper, if you will, coming from Forsyth Street. Traveling outside your street was a risk, but you couldn't spend your whole life on one block, could you?

I didn't want to wait for Fink to gather the Hester Streeters and come after me, so I ran away. After a few blocks, when the pain in my hand had disappeared, I let myself remember how grand it was to plant a good one on Fink. Wait until I told Manny!

EXTRA! EXTRA!

Manny was already hawking papers when I got to Broadway and Fourteenth Street, and there was no time to talk.

"Extra! Extra! Read all about it! Europe laid waste! Thousands dead! Read all about it!" he shouted, attracting a crowd of buyers who eagerly exchanged pennies for newspapers.

I squeezed past the people until I was pressed against Manny and said, "Sorry I'm late."

"Forget it and sell papers!" He pressed a couple dozen copies into my hands.

I'd wave a newspaper in the air, and in a blink, somebody would snatch it away and shove a coin into my open palm.

"Europe beset by death and destruction! Read all about it!" Manny yelled.

Beset by death and destruction? Manny was outdoing himself today. He'd say just about anything to sell a paper. *Ship sinks! Building burns! Maiden outraged!* He loved

4

making up headlines. I think he was practicing for when he became a reporter, which was his dream. I remembered the time he yelled, "Army defeated! Many casualties!" Manny had turned a sports story about the Army baseball team, when a couple of players got brained, into a pearl of a headline. People were steamed afterward when they figured the truth, but Manny sold three dozen papers that day.

"Europe laid waste? Thousands dead? Geez," I said.

"Those are the headlines. No joke! People in Germany are dying left and right," Manny said. "Cholera."

"Cholera!" I repeated, and shuddered. "Crappin' yerself to death ain't no way to die."

The papers and coins flew, and it wasn't long before my stack of papers got thin.

"We need more papers," I said to Manny.

"Gimme yer money and I'll get some more," he replied.

Manny handed his remaining copies to me, took the money, and raced off, all long legs and loose limbs like a baby giraffe. It always made me laugh to watch him run, but the thought of losing a customer kept me from enjoying the sight and returned me to business. I lifted a copy of the paper into the air and shouted, "Read all about it! Death and destruction!"

I did a brisk business, but not as good as Manny had. It was his voice, I decided. You can't help listening to it.

You can hear every word, clear and sharp. I guess it came naturally to him—Manny's voice was like his father's. His father was the cantor of a synagogue on Ludlow Street.

I was down to a couple of copies when Manny returned with a dozen more. "That's all I could get," he apologized, handing me half his stack.

We could have kicked ourselves when we sold out in minutes and watched our customers drift away to other newsboys.

"Look at that. Thems our customers!" I cried. "Why couldn't ya get more papers, Manny?"

"Whadaya think, we're the only newsies looking to get more copies? All the guys were begging Hanratty fer more!" Manny replied.

He pouted and his head fell over like the end of a wet rope. Right away, I was sorry for being sharp with him. Hadn't he sold papers without me when I was late? It was like I'd kicked a puppy.

I wanted to say I was sorry but couldn't find the words. Instead, I said, "Hanratty! I'm surprised the *World* hasn't caught on to that thieving mug."

The filthy slob distributed Pulitzer's paper, the *World*. We'd pay Hanratty a nickel for every ten copies of the paper and then turn around and sell them on the street for a penny a paper. Sometimes, when the headline was real juicy and everybody wanted to buy a paper, Hanratty would hold us up for six cents for ten copies or make us buy a busy location to hawk them, like near a ferry terminal or the stairs to the El, the elevated railroad. And don't think the extra money found its way back to Mr. Pulitzer and the *World*—the only wallet that got fatter was Hanratty's.

Still, selling papers was a great racket, as long as you unloaded all the copies you bought. Unsold copies were the newsie's problem.

"Hey, Hanratty, can ya buy back the unsold copies?" we joked as he drove by in the delivery wagon.

"Take it up with Jew Pulitzer," Hanratty sneered.

"Whadaya mean by that?" Manny said, his hair all up at the low talk against Jews. Manny never took guff from anybody for being Jewish. I wasn't keen on low talk either, but having both Irish and Jewish sides, each getting their share of foul words, my feelings were thicker skinned than Manny's were.

Hanratty just waved his hand toward us as he headed to Park Row and the news offices.

"Miserable mug!" Manny growled.

He found a newspaper sheet and used it as a mitt to pick up an old, hard horse turd. He started to fling it at Hanratty when I said, "Hold it. I got a better arm than you."

Taking the turd, I reared back and let it fly.

The turd flew in a long arc until it hit the wagon and

exploded, spraying a fine, stinking dust over a hulking passerby.

"Watch yer driving!" the man shouted, confusing the dickens out of Hanratty, who hadn't seen or heard the turd bomb.

"Soak yerself! There's nothing wrong with my driving!" Hanratty bellowed.

Me and Manny horse-laughed at the two of them.

"I hope Hanratty gets his nose busted!" Manny guffawed.

They were still shouting at each other as we split the day's profits, each of us taking forty cents. Afterward, I said, "Let's go to Rutgers Square. We can get something to eat and sit by the fountain."

As we walked, I thought about my run-in with Fink and told Manny. I ended the story and said, "Fink stinks. Has since he got off the boat. Remember how he stank of piss and rot?"

"Everybody smells that way off the boat. It's from being cramped up so long," Manny reminded me.

"Yeah, well, he stank worse."

Manny let me burn for a bit, then asked, "Did ya hear he joined the Squab Wheelmen?"

"As a rider or a pickpocket?" I asked.

"A rider. Fink's meaty mitts could never pick a pocket. They're only good for fighting."

At Canal Street, we ducked into a kosher delicatessen

and bought broken cake, paying a penny for a small paper bag of bits from the bottom of a barrel. Then we made our way to the small round Rutgers Street fountain to nibble the sweets.

I worried about being jumped by someone and swiveled my head back and forth. Manny noticed my squirrelly behavior and said, "Relax, Sam. Nobody's gonna thump ya as long as I'm around. I still got friends here."

He made me feel better and the cake tasted even better. We ate quietly until Manny asked, "Did ya read the *Forward*?"

"Nah. You know I'm not much of a newspaper reader," I replied.

"How are ya gonna know what's going on in the world, if ya don't read the paper?" he responded.

"I got you, Manny," I said.

Manny nodded. "There was this letter to the editor from a girl whose father was a cantor . . ."

I listened to Manny tell the story of the unhappy girl and her strict father and how the man lectured the girl for not being an observing Jew. It was Manny's favorite subject, him living through the identical heartache. Manny wanted to become a newspaperman and work the Police Beat, and his father, a religious man, couldn't stomach the thought of it. The two of them fought like cats and dogs.

I had heard Manny's bellyaching many times before,

but I didn't complain; Manny was my friend and I figured a friend deserved a sympathetic ear.

Then someone shouted, "Ya damn fools! Look where yer going. Ya coulda killed me!"

I looked up.

It was the notorious Izzy Fink.

The Pickpockets

Fink shouted, "Ya idiots!"

A pink-faced man, a round woman, and Fink were in a pile on the sidewalk atop a beat-up bicycle. Izzy popped to his feet and screamed, "Ya fools! Ya idiots!"

Yer the only idiot, Fink, ya clumsy oaf, I said to myself. I guessed my punch to his head hadn't slowed him down. It was clear he'd ridden the bicycle into the man and woman. I had a mind to teach Izzy some manners, but Manny's hand went to my shoulder and held me back.

"Squab Wheelmen," he said, grim.

I turned toward the scene of the accident and saw it for what it was, a Squab Wheelmen's dodge. Fink had crashed his bicycle into the innocent couple and sparked a fight to divert attention from Fink's pickpocket pals.

Fink screamed at the dazed couple. The onlookers pressed together to gawk, some people giggling, while others stood open-mouthed. They all were hypnotized by the commotion, and none noticed the half-dozen boys snaking through the crowd.

Those mugs had soft touches, they did, and they picked pockets as easily as taking pickles from a barrel. Lifted wallets and purses were quickly passed to another boy, who dropped them into his pants, where, I guessed, there was a large, secret pouch. It was a common trick— the pickpocket unloads the loot in a blink, in case a wised-up victim accuses him of theft. Without the wallet or purse, the charge can't stick.

"Why didn't youse watch where youse were going!" Fink barked, keeping up his end of the dodge.

Then the pink-faced man, having got his wits back, shouted, "You crashed into us!"

"Yer lyin'!" Fink yelled.

"Guttersnipe!" the man replied, and the onlookers pressed closer.

"Leon, come away!" cried his companion.

On the fringes of the crowd, a pimply-faced pickpocket calmly removed a woman's purse. Another boy roughly jostled a businessman, while a second boy lifted the man's coattails and plucked a wallet from his back pocket.

Another dropped a few pennies on the pavement and said to a nearby man, "Ya dropped yer money."

The man smiled at the youngster's apparent good deed, patted him on the head, and bent over to pick up the pennies. As he did, the boy relieved the man of his fat wallet.

"There's not a Hester Streeter in the bunch," Manny said, and I nodded. I didn't recognize any of the pickpockets as members of Fink's gang. I guessed Fink was splitting his time with a new crop of mugs.

"Slob!" yelled Fink.

"Lowlife!" answered the man.

"Leon, get away!" begged the woman, pulling the pink-faced man. "Let's find the police."

Leon ignored his companion and rushed Fink, with hands outstretched, in a bid to grab him. But Fink easily slipped the man's grasp, laughing cruelly.

"Ya fat slob! Ya couldn't grab yer nuts in yer own pants!" Fink taunted.

Leon's face flushed and he made another stab at Fink. And missed again.

"Hah!" Fink roared.

As Leon tried a third time, the woman grabbed hold of his coattail and tried to hold him back.

"Leon, you're behaving like a common street brawler! Call the police!" she pleaded as he dragged her forward toward Fink. Leon shook her loose and went for Fink, who planted his boot into Leon's knee, sending the man to the ground with a howl. The woman shrieked.

Fink hopped on his bike and pedaled off. The pickpockets disappeared in the hubbub. The onlookers went back to their business. After a few moments, Leon allowed himself to be led away by the woman.

"Slick job," Manny said. Him wanting to be a police-beat reporter, Manny fancied himself an expert on the ways of crooks and gangsters.

I shot him a sour look.

"Gee, Sam, I'm not siding with the Wheelmen, I'm just saying ya gotta admit they did a swell job with the dodge," he said.

I just scowled.

Manny sighed, and said, "Yeah, I know. It's all about Fink and when yer Ma—"

"Just forget about it!" I snapped.

After a few moments of silence, Manny pointed to my half-filled paper bag of broken cake and asked, "Are ya gonna finish that? Cause if ya aren't, I will."

"Oh, I'm gonna take it home. Maybe my pop will want it," I mumbled.

"Yer not going home now, are ya? We could go down to Park Row. I know some police reporters for the *Journal*. We could tag along with them. Maybe there's been a murder. They promised they'd let me see a dead body. That would be swell, wouldn't it?" he asked.

"Yeah, that sounds swell, but I gotta go home."

"Sure thing, Sam. I understand. If I see a dead body, I'll tell ya all about it. Ya wanna sell papers tomorrow? We could try Thirty-fourth Street. By the ferry. Whadaya think?"

"Sure," I said.

I left Manny at Rutgers Square. I shoulda been in a grand mood, what with money in my pocket and sweets in my belly, but I wasn't.

That damn Izzy Fink filled my head as I headed home.

KICKING THE CORPSE

"The lowlife," I mumbled to myself. "Stinking mug."

I was swimming in curses for Fink, when the cries of a nearby delivery wagon driver grabbed my attention.

"Git, Muffin, git," the driver called, his voice all strawberries and cream, trying to encourage the listless animal to pull the green dray she was harnessed to. Muffin's head drooped, her tail twitched, and her glassy eyes blinked.

"Come on, ole girl, you can do it," the driver said, as if speaking to a person. The man was as shiny with sweat as Muffin was.

"Come on, ole girl," the driver repeated in a low, choked voice. "Git along, sweetheart."

Muffin ignored the man and the rustling of the reins that joined man and horse. The man's shoulders fell and he seemed to sink into the wooden wagon bench. He stared at Muffin, shook his head, and screwed up his face in puzzlement. He got no sympathy from the crowd on the street. They kept their attention glued to the wares of the pushcart vendors lining the sidewalk: buckets, bananas, brooms, buttons, bread, and on and on.

The man turned back to the horse and, in a fit, hollered, "Enough is enough. Move!"

With that, Muffin collapsed to the pavement in a heap. Dead.

"Oh, God, no!" the man howled, and leaped from the wagon. His face was twisted and red, a mask of shock and sorrow. Passersby turned their heads toward the hullabaloo, but they turned away when they realized it was just a dead horse and not a real tragedy.

"No, Muffin, no!" the man blubbered, his hands still holding the leather harness straps. "Oh, Muffin, I'm sorry. I kilt you."

Tears rolled down his face and he wore the most pitiful expression. Onlookers chuckled. I felt awful for the man. That horse was probably the man's closest friend and had shared more of the man's life than any human being had. I figured the man had a right to mourn. I was going to tell him so, tell him that it was just Muffin's time and that he hadn't killed her, when the man, all of a sudden, threw down the reins and booted the carcass with a heavy kick.

"Ya miserable beast!" he spat, kicking the corpse a

second time and slapping the side of his wagon. Then he turned away and waded into the crowd, until it swallowed him up like it had Fink earlier.

People are queer-acting creatures, I said to myself, puzzling over the driver's tears and anger. But I didn't puzzle too long when I remembered that hair rings could be woven from a horse's mane. And a dead horse didn't complain when you pulled out the hairs.

I sat down on the base of her neck where it met her shoulders and examined the coarse hairs there, long things colored brown and yellow. Passersby paid dead Muffin little mind. She might lie there for days before she was hauled away.

A fly tickled my nose. I brushed it away. The flies were gathering now, especially around Muffin's tail, where something foul was leaking. I ignored them and plucked the prettiest mane hairs I could find. With each yank, I apologized to Muffin for the damage I was doing to her.

As I twisted the hairs into a pinky ring, a voice called, "Boy, what are you doing?"

I looked up. A man in a proper suit stared at me through wire-frame glasses. He had the high-tilted chin of a man who was used to being listened to. Beside him stood another man, wearing a wide frown beneath a crescent-shaped mustache.

I twisted another plucked hair into position and

ignored him. Why should I bother with some mug who didn't even know my name?

"You, boy, what do you think you're doing?" the voice demanded.

Who was this schmuck?

"Making a ring. A horsehair ring," I said. But I couldn't let his cheek pass unchallenged, and added, "What's it to ya anyway?"

"Biggs, this street Arab isn't worth your time. Let's go," said the second man, speaking with an odd lilt that made me guess he was foreign born. He narrowed his eyes and sneered. But the first man, Biggs, ignored the warning and stepped closer to me.

"What's it to me? Simply, my life. I'd prefer not to be killed by you," he said without a shred of humor.

I had no notion of what he meant and just blinked stupidly.

Biggs looked about for a moment and then pointed to the nearby curb, where a pile of gray-brown horse dung lay in the gutter. Shiny green flies flocked to it

He pointed and said, "If I asked you to sit in that manure, what would you say?"

"I'd say, soak yerself, that's what I'd say," I replied, jutting out my chin.

"Of course you would. Any dunce can understand the foulness of it. But what if I were to tell you that the dead horse you are astride is as foul as the dung, maybe more foul; that it is the home of the filthiest and most danger-ous of creatures, things that would snatch your life away and when they were finished with you, would take my life as well. What would you say to that?"

I looked down at Muffin and along her flanks to her tail and said, "I'd say, 'If there are dangerous creatures, they must be invisible, 'cause I don't see anything.'"

The second man cried, "God, Biggs, we have more important business than educating this, this—"

"Yes, in a sense they are invisible," Biggs said.

I looked at Biggs hard, searching his face for bunk or humbug. But I didn't see any, so I eased up off of dead Muffin. Ambling toward the man, I held the hair ring up to my eye with a bit of fanfare. And there I stood, in front of the two men, admiring my handiwork.

"Let's have a look," said the man, putting out his hand.

"My God, Biggs, this is far too much!" cried his com-panion sourly.

I dropped the ring into Biggs's hand. He held it between forefinger and thumb, scrutinized it with nar-rowed eyes, and then fingered the strands of hair.

After judging for several moments, he said, "It's fine work. Would you consider selling it? How about a nickel?"

My eyes widened in surprise. Who would have thought that a swell like him would have such a great interest in a horsehair ring that he would want to buy it? I nodded. Biggs reached into his pocket and removed a nickel, held the coin above my open palm. But instead of dropping it, he stopped.

"But there is a codicil to our transaction," he said as the nickel hovered beyond my possession.

Codicil? Transaction?

He saw my puzzled face and said, "There is more to our deal than the simple exchange of coin for ring. Along with the ring, the nickel buys your promise to no longer use dead horses as benches."

I thought for a moment and replied, "That would require ten cents, I think."

Laughter exploded from him, and he continued to chuckle as he reached into his pocket for another nickel.

"Done!" he said, letting the two coins fall into my hand.

"Biggs, I can't believe you let yourself be extorted by this tenement thief!" said the other man, but Biggs dismissed his protest with a wave of his hand.

I snapped, "I'm no thief, mister! We made a deal and I struck a hard bargain. Ya don't got no right to insult me!"

Biggs tut-tutted my anger, patted my back, and said, "Don't get your hair up, boy. Mr. Riis misspoke and I apologize for him. But don't be hard on him. He's a great man and has done wonderful things for you and children like you."

"His help must be like the dangerous animals ya mentioned before," I answered. "'Cause it's invisible to me."

Laughter burst from him again, revealing a fine collection of white, regular teeth. He removed his glasses and wiped his eyes.

"See ya," I said. As I trotted toward home, I wondered what kind of business a swell like Biggs might have on the Lower East Side.

MA AND POP

On Grand Street, I bought corned beef, cabbage, potatoes, and carrots, figuring I could boil up the mess and serve it to Pop. It was his favorite dinner. He used to joke with Ma and pretend he didn't like her best Irish dish. He'd say to her, "*My* mother never served me anything like this." And Ma would reply, "Well, until your ma is willing to deliver your dinner from Russia, you'll eat what I put in front of you." They'd both laugh, and my mother would ladle an extra portion of cabbage onto his plate.

He loved to make her laugh, joking about the food or mimicking the swells and mugs of the neighborhood. His best act was pretending to be Smits, the landlord, copying perfectly every tilt of his swelled head, bend of the arm, and twitch of his pig nose. Ma would clap her hands and tell Pop burlesque was the poorer for his absence.

He'd been making her laugh from the first time they met on Rivington Street, where Ma was hawking buttons from a pushcart. I'd heard the story often.

Pop, a smooth-faced young man with the complexion

of sour milk, asked her, "Might you have a small bone-colored button to replace the one that has disappeared from my shirt collar?"

She obliged him, as she did the next day when he returned and requested a tortoiseshell button. Five days and five buttons later, Pop invited Ma to lunch at a Delancey Street deli.

"But I don't even know your name," she said.

"Ira Glodsky," he replied.

"So, you're a Jew?" she asked.

"My rabbi tells me so," he said.

"I'm Irish. Catholic . . . ," she replied, her voice trailing off.

"And Irish Catholics are against lunch?" he asked. She laughed.

They shared a potato knish afterward.

I got home to a busy apartment. Pop sewed beside a table piled high with garments. The Taub brothers, boarders we took in to share the rent, were pressed into the corner of the room, sewing vests. They were new to America, greenhorns from Poland, who were tailors like Pop. Another boarder, Fishblatt the rabbi, sat by the window, smoking, while he drank black tea and read the *Jewish Advance* newspaper.

He might be a rabbi, but he didn't seem so holy to me. The few pennies he earned pounding Hebrew into the heads of a few thick-skulled tenement boys went mostly for beer at Brodie's Saloon or McGurk's Suicide Hall.

I boiled up dinner real good, at least I thought I did. Spooning some onto a plate, I carried it to Pop.

"Dinner," I said.

Pushing aside garments covering the table, I set down the meal. Pop, puffy-eyed from work, kept sewing. I waited a few moments for him to start, feeling stupid just standing there. He shoveled a few spoonfuls of dinner into his mouth, quickly swallowed, and pushed away the plate.

Later, I ate out of the pot but didn't have much appetite.

Afterward, I carried the dirty plates and pots down to the black sink on the ground floor of the tenement. Mrs. Kapinski was cleaning diapers and I had to wait a half hour for my turn to scrub the pots.

Back upstairs, I made my bed: two straight-backed chairs together nose-to-nose so that their seats made a long bench, covered with a heavy blanket.

"'Night, Pop," I said.

He stopped sewing, his endless sewing, and looked up, but just for a moment, the way you do when you glance at a passing shadow—quickly, carelessly. Then he returned to his buttonholes. I closed my eyes and fell asleep to his heavy breathing and the whispering sweep of his fingers sewing.

Pennies and Nickels

I hit the bricks early the next morning. I figured Cohen's coal wagon would be making early deliveries and, if I was lucky, I could snag coal that fell from the wagon.

On the way, I bought a slice of hallah bread from a pushcart and folded it around a piece of corned beef that I had carried from home. It was a swell breakfast, but a little dry, and I wished I'd had some mustard and a pickle to go with it.

Cohen's wagon was on Allen Street, rolling jerkily over the cobblestones. With each jolt, a rock of coal fell from the wagon. This is gonna be sweet action, I said to myself, and chased toward it at a trot.

Suddenly, two colored boys appeared between me and the free coal. Them just coming out of nowhere surprised me and stopped me dead in the middle of the traffic-choked street. A beer wagon bore down on me. Its teamster yelled, "Move it, slob!"

He steered his horses one way and I leaped the other.

"Next time, I'll run ya down!" he shouted.

"Soak yerself!" I hollered back.

A stream of tobacco juice flew from his mouth into the gutter near me. I thumbed my nose. When I looked back at the coal wagon, I saw that a third colored boy had joined the other two, a thick-shouldered fella who looked like he knew how to swing a pick, shovel, or hammer. He stood between me and the coal wagon, his arms folded, his eyes pinned to me like a bird's on a worm, while his pals gathered fallen coal into a cloth sack.

Me and the colored kid stared at each other, trying to send each other silent, scary messages with our eyes, until I thought, This is damned silly, so I smiled, lifted my cap, and bent over like an actor taking a bow. The colored boy just sneered.

"Ya got no sense of humor!" I shouted.

I pulled my cap back on and headed uptown. With no chance of lifting coal, I needed some other way to make money. I headed to the stables on Twenty-fourth Street. Maybe there were a few cents to be made shoveling horse shit.

When I got to Fiss, Doerr, and Carroll's, the horse sellers, three boys were already standing beside its wide double doors. I joined the group and received short, evil glances from the others. I gave them a nasty look in return and held my ground—I had as much right as them to angle for work. A moment later, a burly stableman with a beard like rusty wire strode out of the doors and gave me and the others the quick once-over.

"You three," he said with a soft Irish accent, pointing to the biggest boys, of which I was one. The discarded boy stomped his foot and gave me a hurt look, him knowing he'd have had the work if I hadn't made a last-moment arrival. I would have apologized, but as he left, he mumbled, "Mick bastard," and stalked off.

Mick bastard? I chuckled at the thought: that half-wit had gotten it half right. I'm no bastard, but I am half Mick.

The stableman tossed me a hay fork and pointed toward a row of empty stables.

It was a stinking hour, mucking out those stables. Me and the two others had to dance to the stableman's tune, and he didn't give us much of a chance to jaw. Still, I learned one of the boys was named Bernie, from Division Street. The other? I couldn't make heads or tails of his name, his English being gawd-awful, him a greenhorn and not in America very long. He was from Armenia, wherever that is.

The stableman paid us a nickel each, so I guess the hard work was worth it. The Armenian kid and me pocketed the money and tipped our caps, but Bernie asked, "Can I ride one of the horses?"

"This ain't Coney Island, kid. Beat it," the stableman grunted, and turned to head back inside.

"I'll pay a penny," Bernie said, which stopped the stableman in his tracks.

A deal was struck, and a few moments later, Bernie was astride a huge gelding named Gunner. He looked grand up there, bareback-riding on Twenty-fourth Street.

"You want a ride aboard Gunner, too, laddies?" asked the stableman, the prospect of more pennies dancing in his mind. But me and the Armenian kid just shook our heads. Swell as it might be, I couldn't throw my pennies away on a lark. I patted the Armenian on the shoulder, waved good-bye to Bernie and Gunner, and headed for Manny.

"By the ferry," Manny had said yesterday, so I made my way to the East River ferry dock. It was crazy there, what with people and wagons smashed together, some trying to get on the ferry while others got off. I waded through the crowd and got tugged and pushed, and I was about to give up and head back downtown, when I heard Manny call, "Sam! Sam! Over here!"

I craned my neck and spotted him shimmied partway up a lamppost. His legs and one arm were wrapped tightly to the pole, and he waved madly with his other hand. I waved back and plowed my way through the throng to him.

"It's a madhouse," he said, having climbed down from the pole.

I nodded and asked, "We gonna hawk papers here?"

"And get our heads busted? Naw, the Dagos own this spot. I figured we'd set up shop on a street near an El station on Third Avenue. That way, we can pitch to their riders and people spilling off the ferry too. Whadaya think?"

I gave Manny the thumbs-up and we headed off to a spot on Thirty-first Street. Hawking papers was never easier. You just had to lift the paper in the air and somebody would snatch it away; we didn't bother to shout the headlines or nothin'. Yup, it was feverish, the demand people had for news. It was still about the cholera epidemic, except the new twist was that a bunch of infected steamships from Germany had dropped anchor in the New York Harbor. Another plague ship had already been sent to Long Island and the Long Islanders rioted at the news.

Me and Manny handed out papers and took pennies in a blur. Then I sold a paper and stuck out my palm for the penny, and instead of the hard, flat coin, I felt something fluffy and nearly weightless. Glancing into my hand, I saw a horsehair ring.

"Hey, what's the dodge?" I growled, and looked up at the cheating customer. And saw Dr. Biggs.

The Deal

Me and Biggs walked toward his office near Bellevue Hospital. Manny left to pester the reporters downtown about some kind of job, him not interested in doctors or hospitals unless there was a chance of seeing a dead body, which there wasn't.

Dr. Biggs treated me to a large pretzel from a pushcart, which was swell of him. He asked whether I had brothers or sisters, of which I had none. Then he asked me about selling newspapers, and I told him about the dodge making up headlines, which made him laugh. Then he told me when he was a kid on a farm, he made extra money helping to bale hay. That was something, to think a swell like Dr. Biggs was once just a farm kid scrambling to make pennies like Manny and me.

"Do you like hawking papers?" Biggs asked.

"Sure," I said. "As much as ya can like work. I mean, it's work."

It struck me crazy to think about liking or not liking work. You got to do it whether you want to or not, so it's like asking, Do you like to breathe or not?

But I didn't have any beef with Dr. Biggs. He seemed to really be interested in what I was saying and would nod after I spoke, like he was giving it the once-over.

Finally, he said, "I'm glad I ran into you, Sam. I think I've got a job for a smart kid like you."

Before I could ask him what the job was, someone yelled, "Biggs! Here!"

It was the Riis guy, waving from the next corner.

"Ah, Jacob," Biggs cried, and we joined him.

Seeing me, Riis asked Biggs, "The boy from yesterday?"

He said it like you'd ask, "Hey, do you know you've got horse crap on your shoe?"

"Yes, I ran into him selling newspapers and realized what great fortune it was," Biggs replied.

"You're joking—"

"No, Jacob. I am not. Our young friend will be of invaluable help—"

"What are youse mugs talking about?" I asked.

Biggs looked at me and said, "You can help us. We are looking for someone. A visiting nurse on the Lower East Side. It's important that we speak with her. We've had no luck tracking her down—"

"Ya mean Miss Deitz?" I asked.

Biggs's eyes widened in surprise.

"Everyone in the Tenth Ward knows Miss Deitz," I explained. "She is in and outta the tenements there every day. Taking care of people."

31

"Then you *can* be of some use. You will find her for us," Riis declared in a manner a hair less prickly than usual.

I thought I might be able to soak Biggs for another nickel, and said, "All right, but there is a codicil to our transaction."

I said it in a highfalutin, joking kind of way. Biggs raised his eyebrows.

"Ya'll buy me lunch if I come," I said.

Laughter bubbled out of him as he swept us down the street. Still, I noticed he never agreed about lunch. I guessed it was okay. He struck me as an honest man.

"Why do ya need to find her?" I asked.

The doctor's expression turned dark. Riis cleared his throat and said, "Let's just say Dr. Biggs needs to consult with her."

"Yeah?" I replied.

Biggs hesitated and said, "Cholera."

"Somebody in the tenements got cholera?" I asked.

I'd seen the newspaper headlines and, cruel as it might have sounded, wished for the cholera to stay on those ships and away from me.

Riis and Biggs blanched. A passing man heard me speak and, with wide eyes, turned to listen. Biggs, seeing this, gripped my elbow and led me away. Riis followed. Their stony expressions kept me silent as we threaded our way through the crowds and street peddlers for nearly a block before Biggs signaled a halt.

"You must watch your tongue. The whole city is on edge about the cholera threat, and thoughtless rumors will only add to the tension," Biggs scolded me.

Riis scowled and barked, "Come, Biggs, we have devoted enough time to this wastrel. We were fools to have taken him into our confidence. Come, time is precious!"

"Wait, Jacob. Time *is* precious. Miss Deitz could be anywhere, and without our young friend here, we might waste hours looking for her," he said.

Riis groaned but didn't disagree.

Biggs turned to me and asked, "It's important to find Miss Dietz immediately. Can you help us? Be truthful."

"But Miss Deitz *does* have something to do with cholera, doesn't she?" I asked.

Biggs eyed the crowds of people streaming around us and whispered, "Perhaps. It will all be clear once we find Miss Deitz. Will you trust me?"

Biggs seemed square enough for me. I said, "I bet she's helping with a newborn baby, the one Mrs. Smythe, the butcher's wife, delivered. I know 'cause Mrs. Smythe paid me a nickel to carry her doctoring bag. The poor baby came out all scrawny and raw, like it had a rash all over and still does, so—"

"Splendid!" Biggs said, interrupting my story, which was a bit upsetting in that I hadn't gotten to the good part, about the father being a gangster.

"There's no time to lose, so take us to her now, young Mister . . . uh, Mister . . . I'm afraid I don't know your name," he said.

"Sam Glodsky," I said.

Riis and Biggs stared at me for moment and then burst out laughing. I was about to storm off at the insult, when Biggs said, "We're sorry, Sam, but you look less like a Sam Glodsky than anyone I can imagine. That mop of red hair, freckles, and pug nose of yours suggest you are more a Kelly, O'Connor, or Doyle. I would have bet the world that you're Irish."

"Oh, I favor my mother's looks. She was Irish. Kate Flynn of County Cork, daughter of Daniel Megan Flynn," I explained.

I led them to Henry Street and a tenement that seemed to squat beside the sidewalk like a giant trash bucket. The gutter outside its front door was knee-high with garbage and horse crap.

DESPERATE PERIL

"Ya seen Miss Deitz?" I asked a kid pitching a stone in a game of marbles. He pointed skyward.

"The roof," I explained to Biggs and Riis. "What with the streets mobbed with people and pushcarts, it's easier and faster to travel from building to building by rooftop."

We pounded up the stairwell and emerged onto the roof of the tenement. A half-dozen children played hopscotch beside a pigeon coop. And there, stepping over the low wall that separates one tenement from another, was a square, solid woman in a long, capelike coat, carrying a black bag.

"There she is," I said, pointing.

"Miss Deitz!" Riis shouted, trotting after her.

Biggs extended his hand as he came up to her, and said, "I'm—"

"Dr. Hermann Biggs," she said, and Biggs's eyes widened in surprise. "I heard you lecture at Bellevue. The Revolution in Clinical Medicine. Fascinating."

"Thank you for your kind words, Miss Deitz. I'm flattered," he said, and shook her hand. "I'm afraid my mission today does not concern Bellevue. Rather, Miss Deitz, I have searched you out as part of my duties as chief inspector of the New York Health Department. My friend Mr. Riis and I—"

"Riis? Jacob Riis?" Miss Deitz interrupted, her voice thick with astonishment. "Jacob Riis, the photographer of *How the Other Half Lives*? My goodness, that book is the locomotive that pulls the entire reform movement in this city."

Riis smiled and did his best to appear embarrassed by her admiration.

Biggs cleared his throat and said, "The city of New York is in desperate peril, Miss Dietz, and it needs your help. I am sure you are aware of the cholera ships in New York Harbor.

"The people on board the ships are desperate to flee. Their friends and family on shore are anxious for them to succeed and will go to any length to help them. The police have foiled all escapes . . . until yesterday.

"A man shimmied down the steamship *Moravia*'s anchor line and into a boat, in which four men waited. The boat then raced off. We learned that the man was an American returning from a business trip. His business? Trading in racing pigeons. Yes, racing pigeons! There is a lively gambling business in the racing of thoroughbred birds. He listed an office on Broome Street on the Lower East Side. The address matches the pet shop of Monk Eastman."

"The gangster? That complicates things, doesn't it?" gasped Miss Deitz.

Biggs continued, "I believe Eastman is hiding the man somewhere nearby. He's getting sicker by the moment and—"

"Come!" Miss Deitz cried, darting away and waving us on.

"What—?" Biggs mumbled.

"Your man. I think I know where to find him," Miss Deitz replied.

"Where?"

"On Rivington. I'll take you there."

We trailed behind her. Biggs and Riis jabbered excitedly at the thought of maybe cracking the nut of their hard problem. Me, I was wondering if Miss Deitz recognized me from before.

BEATEN DOWN AND CHASED OFF

The weather that summer had been agony. Every day was mad-dog hot, so sweltering that it could drive the sanity from man or beast. The river offered the only relief, but the Micks controlled the riverfront and they guarded their treasure closely. Jewish and Italian gangs tried to shoehorn their way in but always failed. I know about the defeats 'cause I had been a soldier in some of the battles. Me and the Forsyth gang had nearly carried the day against the Micks until they rained cobblestones down on us from the rooftops and threw us back.

Them falling cobblestones made a horrible clattering racket when they hit the street. It scared the tar out of me. *Bang! Bang! Bang!* Like the Devil banging a drum. Defeating the riverside Micks wasn't worth getting brained, I said to myself, and quit the gang the next day.

My mother was thrilled; she hated the gangs awful. "Blockheads in concert," she called 'em.

But then a wave of broiling heat tortured the city like a punishment from God. It killed horses and old people. It was the Fires of Hell, and after a few days, I had to have a swim or lose my mind. T'hell with the Micks, I told myself, and marched toward the river, where I planned to install myself in waters beside the Jackson Street beach. I headed east and plunged into Irish territory.

My courage soon evaporated like horse piss in the gutter. My heart was in my throat and my senses were strung tight for danger. With every step, I expected someone to shout "Yid!" and pile on. I kept my head low and avoided people's eyes. But after a while, I realized something strange: No one paid me the slightest mind, and I arrived at the river ignored, and in short order. Not giving my good fortune a second thought, I tore off my shirt and dived into the river. I dog-paddled around; it was the only swimming stroke I had mastered during rare visits to Coney Island. A dozen Irish boys splashed and dunked each other nearby. I didn't come out of the water until the skin on my fingers wrinkled.

As I gathered my shirt from the beach, I noticed a big blond kid eyeing me. The hairs on the back of my neck stood to attention and my heart pounded. Oh well, I thought, the swim was worth a thrashing. Brave words but without weight, for in my heart of hearts, I was desperate to avoid a dustup where I'd be outnumbered twelve to one. I was sashaying away, trying my best to mask my fear by affecting a nonchalant air, when I heard someone call, "Hey, laddie!"

I kept walking.

"Hey, laddie!" the voice repeated.

A hand gripped my shoulder and spun me around. It was the blond kid.

"Are ya deaf or sumtin'?" he bawled.

Behind him were two more Micks. I expected a smash or a pile-on, but the trio just looked at me. I couldn't think of anything to do except shrug my shoulders.

"Ya new here, laddie?" asked the blond.

I nodded.

"Well, then, ya need a gang. Without a gang, the Yids and Eyeties will jump ya. Can't be havin' that, can ya? Join up with us and ya can tell them others to soak themselves. How's that? Are ya in?" asked the boy, who then reached out his hand for me to shake. "My name's Malachy."

Here I was expecting a fist in the face, and instead, there was Malachy waiting for our hands to join. I stared at that hand floating in space for what seemed to be forever as I tried to figure the dodge.

Then it struck me: Apart from our hair color and my slighter build, Malachy and me looked alike. Not only had he and the others not recognized me as one of the Yids from the Forsyth Streeters, they mistook me for a full-blooded Irishman! Why nobody had noticed it before was a mystery, and the best I could figure was that it was something that I'd grown into. However it happened, I didn't really care, what with it letting me slip by without a beating. So I took Malachy's hand and, recalling my grandfather, said, "I'm Danny Flynn."

Joining the Jackson Street gang was a sweet deal. On hot days, I'd go over to the river and take a swim. The fellers, they were grand to me and we had high times. They never seemed to notice that I was always absent for serious gang business, like jumping kids from Forsyth Street. But I was no fool and knew the risk of being unmasked. I counted on ending my Jackson Street hijinks at the close of summer.

What I hadn't figured was Mrs. Smythe, the butcher's wife, spotting me hobnobbing with Malachy and his mob, the very thieves leeching protection money from Mrs. Smythe's husband. She noted my presence, reckoned I was part of the gang, and promptly informed my mother.

"You're back in a gang?" Ma hollered. "Have you lost all good sense or did it leap from your head like a goat from a rock?"

The summer heat was a spring breeze compared to the furnace of her anger.

"Quit the gang, Samuel, or I'll come down there and drag you away by your ear!" she warned.

Ma's anger being so keen, I knew she wouldn't sit still for no explanation about me being something of a fair-weather gang member, so I swore I'd quit. And I did, swearing off East River swims for weeks afterward. Then the first week of September arrived with a spell of heat that melted my promise into vapor.

I sneaked back to the Jackson Street beach. The gang greeted me like the Prodigal Son, clapping me on the shoulder and laughing. Where ya been? they asked. Workin' as a telegraph delivery boy, I said, and they swallowed the lie whole. Then it was into the water, where we splashed for the remainder of the afternoon.

We were coming out of the water, when someone shouted, "Yids!" and a mob of kids swooped down from the street screaming curses, tossing rocks, and swinging fence slats. I spied Izzy Fink among the attackers—we'd been set upon by his Hester Street gang.

The Jackson Streeters scattered. Me and Malachy retreated to the stoop of a grimy, abandoned waterfront building. Two of the Hester Streeters came flying at us, but we beat them down and chased them off.

"There's a pile of cobblestones on the roof. Don't let 'em up there or it'll be raining rocks!" Malachy said.

"I'll hold the door shut!" I cried.

Malachy joined the battle on the street and I raced into the tenement, slamming the door shut and jamming myself against it.

In a blink, some Hester Streeters tried to tear open the door. It was an awful tug-of-war keeping it closed, but I kept a hard grip. The entire Hester Street mob screamed and cursed. I picked out Fink's voice from the others. It was easy, what with him so hot at the stuck door.

"Ya damn Mick! I'm gonna bust yer head! Bust it!" he screamed. But he still couldn't get the door open. I coulda split a gut laughing, him not never catching on that it was me.

But after a while, the extra hands on the other side took a toll on my strength and the door cracked open. Then it flung wide, taking me with it, and I got thrown onto the sidewalk and into a brawl. It was a punching and kicking pile after that, but I still caught a glimpse of Fink racing past me and into the building with a bunch of his pals.

I wish I'd chased after him.

Pretty soon, Malachy and some of the boys pulled a couple of mugs off me and then headed for the roof. The cobblestones came raining down soon after, and the clang of falling stones was everywhere. Everybody, Hester Streeters and Jackson Streeters alike, dived for the tenement entrance to avoid the stones, bringing the fight into the building. We were going at it pretty good, punching, shouting, and cursing.

Suddenly, there was a scream outside.

Then cries of help rang out. Something shocking and awful had happened, more shocking and awful than a thrashed kid.

Afterward, when I knew, I wasn't sure who to blame: Mrs. Smythe for spotting me again and singing to my mother, or Fink and the Hester Streeters for starting the brawl. In the end, I blamed myself. If I had held the door, the Hester Streeters wouldn't have made it to the roof to toss cobblestones. But most of all, it was my fault for breaking my promise to Ma and ignoring her threat to drag me home by my ear. I couldn't shake the logic of it: If she hadn't come to collect me from the Jackson Street gang, then she wouldn't have got killed by a cobblestone tossed from the roof. It was my fault, and the truth of it made my heart fly apart in a million directions.

But I didn't get the chance to feel sorry for myself, because Pop shattered.

He and Ma had defied friends and family to marry—a Jew and a Catholic—and the world exiled them for it, shipwrecking them to the tiny island of their love. Now she was gone and he was marooned. And don't try to say I was a comfort to him, 'cause a son ain't a wife and any idiot could see the difference.

He slept all the time and stank from his own filth. He stopped eating and drinking. I couldn't coax a word, a smile, a nod from him. It was suicide and I was terrified.

Then Manny delivered Miss Dietz to me. "She's a nurse. Fer yer old man," he explained.

With sweet words and a tender touch, Miss Dietz held Pop to this world. But he escaped only immediate death, trading it for a living death. He rarely ventured from the tenement, rarely spoke, and filled his hours sewing buttonholes for pennies.

It had been a year.

MY GRAND IDEA

"How's your father?" Miss Deitz asked, surprising me that she remembered at all.

I said, "The same."

She patted my hand and gave me a sad, knowing smile. Then she turned to Biggs and Riis, who followed behind, and said, "I learned of a sick man this morning. He was dead when I arrived."

"Dead?" Biggs repeated.

"Damn!"

"Then we are too late. We can learn nothing here," Riis said.

"Perhaps. Perhaps not," Dr. Biggs replied.

We dodged the pedestrians and the pushcarts, the hansom cabs and the trolleys.

"This way," said Miss Deitz, and she led us down the street and delivered us to a grimy tenement.

Outside stood three cops. One of them strode up to us and waved us away.

"G'day, Miss Dietz. Got orders. Nobody's to enter," he

said with a thick Irish brogue. Another cop removed his billy club.

"This is Dr. Biggs, Sean," explained Miss Deitz. "He is with the Health Department."

Miss Dietz's word seemed good enough for the copper, who nodded and took a step back.

"I never considered cholera. Foolish of me, since there are five cholera-ridden ships in the harbor. The diagnosis should have leaped into my mind—it was quite awful," she said, shuddering a bit, her eyes darting between Riis and Biggs.

"Diagnosis can be tricky for even the finest doctor. Don't punish yourself," Biggs offered, his voice as smooth as cream. "Do we know anything about him?"

Miss Dietz shrugged and turned to the copper, who had stayed within earshot.

"Gormann. A young man, about thirty. The landlord said he took to bed yesterday afternoon. Complaining of a lousy gut and terrible cramps in the joints. Neighbors heard him moaning for hours during the night. Then nothing. The landlord found the body," Sean said.

"Had he been abroad recently?" Biggs asked.

"Abroad? I'd think not," she said. "He was a plasterer's helper. Not the sort to travel."

"Are you certain?" Biggs asked.

If the dead man had been a working stiff, then I figured he wasn't our guy.

"Dead certain. His boss arrived here earlier, inquiring

of him. Said Gormann left work early yesterday with a rotten stomach," Miss Deitz added.

"How might a plasterer's helper have been infected with cholera?" Biggs wondered grimly.

"The landlord said the man received packages from Germany. He had family there. Perhaps there was something in the packages that afflicted him," the copper offered.

"We'll never really know," Biggs muttered.

"I'm sorry for the wild-goose chase. Your sick man from the ship is still out there. If he's not dead already," Miss Dietz noted.

"And those who sailed out to the ship to help make the man's escape might be infected as well," Biggs added.

"They'll bring the disease to their wives and children, and the number could jump until New York becomes Hamburg," Miss Dietz said in a hollow tone. "I'm sorry. I wish I could be of more help, but I must go. There are people who need me. I promise I won't make the same mistake and overlook a case of cholera. Good luck."

Biggs thanked her and she walked off.

"I guess we should keep searching," Biggs said.

We stood there, sagging beneath the weight of the long odds against us. A pile of horse dung in the gutter caught my eye. An enormous cloud of flies buzzed above it. An idea jumped into my head.

I said, "The men can be anywhere, and it would take us till doomsday to search every alley—"

"We know that already, Sam, " Biggs replied.

47

"So this is what I'm thinking," I continued. "It's like trying to follow a horsefly down Tenth Avenue—nearly impossible, right? So instead of chasing the fly, wouldn't it be smarter to just wait by a load of manure till the fly shows up?"

"I'm not sure if I understand you, Sam," Biggs replied.

"The sick man and the mugs who sailed out to the *Moravia*, what do they have in common? What is their pile of horse crap?"

Biggs's face screwed up in puzzlement.

"Monk Eastman!" I said. "The sick guy was in Germany on an Eastman errand, and I bet the friends and boatmen take orders from Eastman, too. The answer is at Eastman's."

"Yes, but Eastman is a common thug who'd laugh in my face if I asked for his help," he replied.

"Who said we have to ask?" I answered, and described my plan.

"No, I don't like it," he said when I'd finished. "I can't ask you to do it. Joining Monk Eastman's gang to learn the whereabouts of the sick man is too dangerous. Your life would be at jeopardy should Eastman discover the truth. And besides, what would possess Eastman to share the information with you?" Biggs said.

As I began to disagree, Biggs signaled *stop* with a lifted hand, but I ignored him and said, "You got a better plan?"

"I can't ask you to take the risk—"

With that, Riis laughed.

"Risk, Dr. Biggs? Sam's whole life has been a risk. It's a miracle he survived his first year and didn't die from measles, chicken pox, scarlet fever, or some other dreadful scourge that whisks children off to eternity. Then there's tetanus, pneumonia, influenza. Or the simple cut that becomes gangrenous. The trolley wheels. A rabid dog. Drowning in the East River. A tenement fire.

"What is Monk Eastman compared to those nasty odds? If he's calculated the risk and finds it acceptable, then who are we to say we know better?"

Biggs stared at Riis for a long time before he said, "All right. Go to Eastman's and find out what you can. I promise more than a free meal for your help. *But be careful!*"

I shook Dr. Biggs's hand and thanked Riis, not an easy thing, what with me having to accept that maybe he wasn't the fathead I'd thought he was.

"How will we stay in touch with you?" Biggs asked.

"I'll find a way," I replied, racing off.

Adventure and money! Didn't this day beat all!

BITING AND CLAWING

I was sure Monk Eastman would have a job for me. Hadn't he tried to hire me before as a lookout?

No, getting in with Monk wouldn't be a problem. But finding the cholera man was a tougher nut to crack. I figured I needed to finagle a job close to Monk himself for that. My mind was working all the angles when I turned onto Broome Street near Monk's place.

Suddenly something hurtled me forward, sprawling me to my face, and my head bounced off the sidewalk. Fireworks of white, red, and yellow lights leaped before my eyes. Hands tore at me, flipping me to my back.

Fink!

Pinned down beneath him, I managed to lift my hands in time to block his punch to my face. He threw another punch, but it bounced off my arm. I shot out my hand and grabbed a handful of hair. Yanking his head down, I took a giant bite out of his ear. Hollering awful, Izzy vaulted backward.

I scrambled to my feet. The sight of the screaming,

bloody-eared Fink shocked his gang, giving me the chance to pop the kid in front of me square in the kisser, knocking him flat. I kicked a third and he crumbled. Then I took aim at another mug as someone jumped on my back, dragging me to the ground. The pile-on followed.

The heap of bodies almost pressed the breath from me. Everyone was biting and clawing to make some room. Then the sharp tom-tom of a policeman's billy club hitting the sidewalk froze us all. It was a cop's signal for help, and the thought of a swarm of cops sent us all running.

I raced for a nearby alley and hid behind a garbage can. Coppers came from everywhere, trapping a bunch of the Hester Streeters and hauling them away. I didn't see Fink among them. I stayed hidden until it was all clear, then went back to the sidewalk and slipped into the crowd. Walking fast, I headed to Monk Eastman's.

A half-dozen sprawled cats lay sunning themselves at the pet store entrance. I tiptoed over them and slipped inside. There were more cats on the floor, on a desk and chair close to the entrance, on the shelves lining one wall. They meowed, spat and cried, and the place stinked of cat piss. The back of the store was divided off by chicken wire. Pigeons cooed from behind the wire, pecking at kernels of seed on the floor or resting on crudely made perches. More cats stood outside the wire, licking their chops and watching the birds.

Everyone knew the joint was more a rescue mission for the animals than a pet store. Strange as it seemed, Monk was an animal lover.

A small, bent man with sunbursts of purple veins on his cheeks appeared. "Whadyawant?" he asked.

"Monk," I replied.

"The roof. Flying the birds," he said, then reached into a barrel of breadcrumbs, grabbed a handful, and threw it at the pigeons. A whirlwind of feathers followed as the birds dashed for the food. I headed to the roof. Five stories later, I found Monk standing with three other men beside a large, freshly painted pigeon coop.

A monster, he was. His enormous back and shoulders stretched the fabric of his coat and partially popped the armpit seams. Atop a thick neck rested a bullet-shaped head, shaved smooth all over. Balanced on his head was a tiny derby. Misshapen cauliflower ears sprouted from the sides of his head. His crooked nose threw a shadow over full lips. Ridges of white scars ran across his knuckles and neck.

The scars, ears, and nose were souvenirs of past battles. He was a tough customer. For fifteen dollars, Monk would chew off a man's ear. Twenty-five bought a broken bone. If you needed someone to be hurtled into the Hereafter, Monk charged a hundred bucks.

But now he was relaxed as he watched his flock of pigeons circle overhead. The birds went around and around, all part of the pigeon keepers' game, in which pigeons were sent aloft, and winning meant gathering birds at the expense of another keeper's flock. I glanced skyward. No other keepers flew their birds. I guessed they had abandoned the air to Monk. You would have had to be nuts to take one of Monk's birds.

One of the birds, a giant dark blue pigeon, broke from the flock and flew to Monk, landing on his shoulder. I'd heard of the pet bird, but this was the first time I had seen it. The bird eyed me closely, reminding me of the hungry cats downstairs.

As Monk fed the bird bits of bread he carried in his coat pocket, he noticed me and waved me over.

"Hey ya, kid, whatcha want?" he asked.

"Looking fer work," I said. "I can do plenty."

I was betting Monk had *something*.

Monk's eyes lifted like he was reviewing an invisible ledger, then he said, "Naw, kid. Ain't no steady jobs any-wherz—"

"I can take care of things, Monk. Take care of people," I said, almost kicking myself for trying too hard to make some kind of connection to the cholera man.

Monk just shook his head, *nope*.

Things weren't looking good. If Monk told me to scram, I'd have to leave and there'd go my chance of finding the infected gangster. I tried to appear sunk, frowning with my head hung low, and said, "Ya sure, Monk? I don't want to go scrambling through the garbage cans like a stray cat."

Mentioning stray cats must have tapped the wee bit of pity in Monk.

He said, "I might have something fer ya. It's a onetime thing, and it ain't easy, but it's worth a few bucks. And if ya duz a good job, who knows. Whadaya say?"

"Depends on what I have to do."

Monk looked around and said, "Best we have this talk in my office."

DEATH SHIP

Monk's third-floor office was cluttered with scruffy chairs, a couple of tattered sofas, and beat-up tables. A half-dozen spittoons stood about, all brimming with the most loathsome green-brown liquid. I guessed Monk used the space to meet with his gang.

Monk collapsed onto a sofa, sending the pigeon gliding from his shoulder to the ground. It began pecking at a half-eaten roll. Monk pulled a cigar from his coat pocket and bit off the tip. He lifted another one and waved it in the air toward me.

"No thanks," I said.

I slipped onto a wooden chair and waited as Monk lit his stogie. Suddenly, the pigeon, with the roll firmly in its beak, leaped into the air and flew back to Monk's shoulder, slapping me across the face with its wing as it passed. I flung myself back in shock and nearly spilled off the chair. Monk hee-hawed with laughter, and exhaled clouds of blue smoke. Still chuckling, he shooed the bird away, and it flew to the arm of a chair across the room. I ducked as it sailed past me.

Monk was silent for a moment, then said, "Howz yer old man?" He knew about Pop, even though they'd never met, like he knew about everything.

I nodded.

"That's grand," he said.

Monk, gangster or not, was something of the neighborhood mayor. He brought in business, protected jobs, and kept everyone safe . . . the way a farmer keeps a chicken safe for future plucking.

Monk stared at me, I guess sizing me up one last time, and then said, "Here's the deal, kid. I needs ya to snatch something fer me," he said.

"Ya sure ya want me, Monk? I bet ya got plenty of guys who can lift stuff fer ya. Better guys than me. The only thing I've ever lifted was potatoes and apples from the pushcarts," I said, not wanting to be part of a wildgoose chase that had nothing to do with finding the cholera man.

"Truly said. But this is a special lift. Being sly is just a part of it. Ya gotta have the right attributes." The last word tumbled out of Monk's mouth sounding like *at-TREE-beauts*.

I wasn't sure what he was talking about, but I nodded knowingly. I figured he would eventually get to the point.

"Ya like birds?" he asked.

Boids.

I nodded. Yes.

"Well, there's nothing grander than a racing pigeon, and the grandest racer in the world was in Germany. Outflew every pigeon from London and Vienna. I wanted that boid awful! Awful! Ya know what I mean? So I bought it. Cost a fortune, but I don't care. Anyway, I sends one of the boys over there to collect it, which he does lickety-split, and then hops a boat home. But, damn the awful luck of it, he's shipped onto one of them cholera ships. Here he is, in New York, bobbing out in the harbor, but the blockheaded health bums won't let him off and, worse luck, won't let me take my boid!"

Mention of the cholera ships got my attention. I leaned forward.

"Well, I am not without my resources, and I arrange to get the guy and the boid off and I does, but the idiot"— *idgit*—"shimmies down the anchor line without the Duke of Prussia."

Duke? I stared blankly at Monk.

"The Duke of Prussia. The boid!"

Oh.

"So, the nitwit shimmies down the line and into our boat—"

"You were there?" I asked.

Monk scowled at the interruption, but nodded he had been there. I wonder, Is Monk infected? Then decided he'd already be sick if he were.

"He falls in the boat without the boid. 'Wherz Duke?'

57

I hollered. 'Left him in the hold,' he sez. Then he starts screaming, 'Get me away from this death ship! Get me away.' Then, all of a sudden, a police department boat is bearing down on us, so we gotta scoot. Widout da boid!" Monk finished the story, red-faced and breathing hard.

"What happened to the guy?" I asked.

"First, I made him tell me exactly where the boid was on the ship, and then he, well . . ."

He paused.

"Then he had an unfortunate accident." *'N fourchinette ax-dent.*

Monk's mouth twisted into an ugly, smug smile. I must have looked shocked or confused, because he quickly added, "Whadya expect? He had a job to do and the mug didn't hold up his end."

The poor mug shoulda been mourned, I guess, but my first thought wasn't of him but of Dr. Biggs. He should be told!

Monk continued, "Soze this is what I'm thinkin'. Me, ya, and a few of the boys head back to the boat soze we can lift the boid. Ya game?"

Lift the bird? I wasn't really sure how he planned to lift the bird from the boat, but I was game—game to get Biggs the information he needed. I nodded.

"Grand! Just grand!" he said. "Come on. I'll introduce ya to the boys. They're just around the corner."

"I Swear! I Swear!"

Just as we were leaving, Herm Levy, a greasy mug in an expensive suit, fourth in command of the Eastman Gang, entered.

"Hey, Monk," he said. "I brung the bag to Big Tim, like ya asked."

Big Tim Sullivan.

There was only one Big Tim: Big Tim Sullivan, a Tammany man. Nothing happened in New York without the Tammany politicians. Big Tim had been a Tammany man for years. He had visited Ma after her father had been killed by a trolley. He told her the funeral would be grand and paid for, to boot. But then he told her to vacate her apartment, explaining it had been bestowed on her father for his good Tammany work and, now that he was gone, would be bestowed on the man who would replace him.

"Have you thought about taking a room?" Big Tim had asked as he boxed Ma's things.

She ended up in a dark and damp basement apartment.

Big Tim Sullivan was never a popular mug in my house.

"Yeah, Big Tim and me talked," Monk said, the edges of his voice hard and sharp, and his eyes narrowed to slits. Something was up. Levy noticed it too and backed away a step.

"There some kinda problem?" Levy asked.

"Ya might say so, Levy. Big Tim said the bag was light," Monk growled.

"Well, Big Tim's wrong. Nobody could have messed with the cash. That bag never left my hand and I delivered it just the way ya gave it to me. I didn't even look inside it. I swear, Monk."

"So ya say."

Monk edged closer to Levy, who kept backing away until he hit the wall and stopped. Monk came nose-to-nose with him and glared down at him. Beads of sweat sprouted from Levy's forehead.

"I swear," Levy murmured. His eyes darted left and right.

"Soze yer saying Big Tim is a liar?" Monk asked. "Would ya like to tell that to Big Tim in person, tell him he's a liar?"

I've seen a rat cornered by a cat, and I swear Levy's eyes had the same panicky look. It was a hell of a fix he was in, what with having to choose between Monk Eastman and Big Tim Sullivan for an enemy. If Levy was smart, he'd throw himself into the East River now and be done with it.

"I'm not saying anybody's a liar, Monk. I'm just saying ya gave me three hundred bucks and I delivered three hundred bucks," Levy cried.

You had to hand it to Levy. He didn't give up.

"Three hundred bucks, ya say. How would ya know there was three hundred bucks cash money if ya never even looked inside?" Monk asked.

It was like the air went out of Levy, the way he seemed to shrink. Monk had caught him lying and that had to be no good.

"I swear, Monk, I didn't take no cash. I swear!" Levy pleaded.

Monk pushed down on Levy's shoulder and shoved him to the floor, sending a couple of cats scrambling away so as not to get squashed. Monk slapped Levy's derby off his head and then clutched him by the neck. The whole time, Levy kept whispering, "I swear. I swear."

This was awful to watch.

Monk steered Levy's head to a nearby spittoon and pushed his face toward the disgusting liquid.

"Ya swear ya didn't take nothing?" Monk barked.

"I didn't take nothin'. Nothin'!" Levy cried as his nose nearly touched the spittoon. "I took the cash out and counted it. That's all! I was just curious! But I put it all back. I didn't take nothing!"

The space between Levy's face and the foul spit was thinner than a cat's hair. I coulda sworn Levy was crying. Then Monk yanked him clear and sent him flying.

"Next time, keep the bag closed! If I wanted ya to know what was inside the bag, I woulda told ya. Otherwise, keep yer snoot outta my business! Got it? Nothing goes on in the Lower East Side without me knowing about it. A pigeon could crap on an awning on Delancey Street and I could tell ya how much and which awning. Don't ever forget that, and don't ever think ya can pull a fast one on me!" Monk yelled.

Levy nodded fast and said, "Sure, Monk. Sure."

"Come on, kid," Monk said, and headed for the door.

He stopped to pick up an orange-and-black tabby that had encircled his legs. The cat purred as Monk ran his hand from the animal's snout to the very tip of its tail. Then, with the tenderness of a mother cat, Monk grasped the back of the tabby's neck and lowered it to the ground.

"I'll Smack Ya!"

I followed Monk to the crowded sidewalk. People stepped aside as we walked, and greeted him. "Hi ya, Monk," or "How are you doing, Monk," or "Afternoon, Monk," they said. Monk nodded slightly or mumbled a greeting in return—nothing big, mind you, just enough to let the person know he'd been noticed. But it was still enough to make them smile wide. What was funny was that *I'd* get a "How-ya-doin'" and a tip of the hat, too. I guessed that something of Monk rubbed off onto me, and it felt grand to be treated so swell.

Monk stopped at Capshaw's Restaurant, a seedy joint popular with Tammany men and gangsters. Being neither, I'd never been inside. Someone had scrawled *Good Eats* in the grime that coated the glass-front window. We ducked inside. A great cloud of cigar smoke filled the place, and I stayed glued to Monk's heels as he walked to the back, afraid if he got too far ahead I'd lose him in the fog. A few diners waved and Monk nodded. He strolled toward a large round table and three people. One of them was Izzy Fink. His ear was raspberry-colored and leaked blood from a half moon of teeth marks.

"I'll smash ya!" Fink spat when he saw me, and leaped from his chair, fist raised.

But Monk clamped his huge, meaty fist around Izzy's arm, lifted him off the ground, and tossed him to one side. Fink crashed into the legs of the chair he had moments before been sitting in.

"Take yer seat, ya brat, and don't make no more trouble," Monk ordered.

Fink clambered up. An onlooker giggled, but Izzy didn't have the stomach to snarl or nothing.

I guessed if it wasn't for Monk, I would have been in one heck of a fight. I didn't say it out loud, but I thanked him something awful.

I slid into a chair beside Monk. I recognized the others: Tilson, the Horse Poisoner, a bald-headed, beady-eyed character. He'd kill your enemy's horse for the right price, a dreadful thing for a man who needed a horse to run his business. The thought of killing horses turned my stomach. Beside him was a small man with fancy clothes, Mike Murphy. He ran a clip joint on Allen Street. He was Italian but used an Irish name, the odds being better for Irishmen than Italians in New York, even in the gangster trade.

Herm Levy showed up a few minutes later and slunk into a chair at the table. Monk didn't give him a high sign or nothing.

The waiter set down schooners of beer and everybody took long swallows, except me. Not liking the stuff, I just sipped a bit of the foam, just to be sociable. Monk wiped his mouth with his sleeve, pointed to me, and said, "This here is Sam Glodsky. He's gonna help us finish the job with the boid. If ya got other ideas, well forget 'em, or take 'em up with me. Understood?"

Everyone knew Monk was talking directly to Fink. We all gave him the side glance and watched him nod, although I thought it was a slow and reluctant one.

Monk lowered his voice and said, "This is the deal. After midnight, we sail outta Brooklyn. Just like last time. Our pal, Chief of Police Devery, promised me he'd yank the police boats but not forever, so we have to be quick.

"Sam and Fink will sneak on the ship. I figure, them being kids, they can do it better than any of us guys. They'll make their way to the ship's hold, where the Duke is stored. I got a map of the ship so the brats'll know exactly where to go."

A sheet appeared from Monk's inner coat pocket and unfolded in front of us. Izzy and I lifted out of our chairs and leaned close to the map to get a good look. A crudely drawn diagram of the ship showed passageways and decks as well as arrows pointing the route to the bowels of the ship, where the pigeon lived. There was a big star drawn there.

Monk traced the route with a sausage-thick finger and murmured, "Ya go here, down there, follow this to the stairwell, and follow it all the way to the bottom and into the holds until ya reach the boid."

"It's a swell plan, Monk," Levy said.

"We got to grab the boid tonight. There's talk that the ship is going to be moved to the outer harbor or Long Island, and who knows if we could make the snatch then. So no slipups. Got it?"

Still, I had a few qualms about Monk's scheme, and asked, "What about the sailors? Won't somebody spot us?"

"Use yer head, kid. Chances are there won't be any guards. Come on, who'd expect somebody to sneak *onto* a death ship?" Monk replied.

It seemed to make sense, so I kept my yap shut. But calling the steamer a death ship almost killed my appetite.

Monk waited for anyone else to put in their two cents, but nobody said nothing. After a moment, he said, "Let's eat."

Minutes later, the waiter was sliding plates of roast beef in front of each of us. Giant slabs they were, swimming in brown gravy and surrounded by a pile of potatoes. It was the grandest beef I'd ever seen, and I started sawing away at it with my knife, cutting bits of it off and stuffing them into my mouth while the others joked about coppers or Tammany Hall blockheads. Well, not everybody. I noticed Fink silently devoured his meal, too.

We all had second helpings of beef before Monk pushed away his plate and stood up.

"I'll expect you guys at the pet store at eleven. Don't be late," he announced, and started to leave, signaling me to follow him out. I mopped up the last bit of gravy on my plate with a bit of bread, stuffed it into my mouth, and followed. Outside, Monk stopped, scratched his belly, and belched.

"I seen ya shoveling it away. Did ya have yer fill?" he asked.

"More than my fill, Monk. Thanks. It was grand, the grandest I've ever had," I said, stretching the truth only about being filled. I could have downed another two plates of beef.

He said, "Listen, there's something I gotta tell ya. Something I couldn't say inside. Fink's like a cellar rat and can find his way outta a tough spot, but he don't have the brains to find the boid. That's where ya come in. I figure between the two of ya, there'll be the right mix of nerve and smarts to get the Duke. But ya'll have to lead the way. Don't let me down."

Monk reached into his pocket and flipped me a coin. As he walked away, he said, "I'm trusting ya."

I looked into my palm and saw a shiny five-dollar Liberty coin.

Sneaking Out

I'd never seen a five-dollar coin before and sure never held one. It kind of hypnotized me, and I stared, half expecting it to start talking to me. I bounced it in my hand, feeling the grand heft of it. Five dollars!

Then the shock of carrying it hit me. It was an awful lot of money, and I snapped my head around and searched for the lowlife among the passing people who might snatch it away from me. I didn't see nothing, just people trudging home with little mind for me. Still, I felt uneasy.

I pressed myself close to Capshaw's and bent down. Pretending to fix my shoelace, I slipped the coin into my shoe and pressed it toward my toes. Then I stood and headed off. As I walked, I felt it bounce against my toes. If it had been a rock or pebble, I would have hated the bumping, but it was a five-dollar Liberty, and I grinned from ear to ear. I thought about the shot to the snoot I'd deliver to anyone who tried to relieve me of the Liberty. How did rich people handle their money? It was plain stupid to think they kept it in their socks.

I headed uptown. There was plenty to tell Dr. Biggs, like how he should call off the search for the man from the ship. Or how Monk and the others should be grabbed because they might be infected. And about the plan to return to the *Moravia*. I headed up toward Bellevue and the doctor.

The tap-tap-tapping of the coin against my toes starting me thinking about how I'd spend it and the grand lark five dollars could buy. No more broken cake for me; I'd buy myself a box of cookies and eat them lazying around the Rutgers Square fountain. Then I'd go back to Fiss, Doerr, and Carroll's stables and buy myself a whole afternoon atop that gelding. I laughed at the daydream of tossing the money away on sweets and horse rides.

Monk had flipped that Liberty five to me like it was no more than a penny. You got to have plenty to toss off five bucks like that. I figured Monk could afford larks that I couldn't even imagine.

What with me needing money so badly and Monk giving it away so easily, why was I in a rush to toss him over to Dr. Biggs, and probably the coppers as well? When Monk went, so would the money.

The five dollars obliged me to board the cholera ship and risk a nasty death. Five dollars are grand, but the wages hardly squared with the danger.

Still . . .

Do this job right and there are probably plenty more jobs on its heels. Before you know it, five-dollar Liberties will be dropping into your hands like raindrops falling from the sky!

The more I thought, the slower I walked, until I came to a dead stop. When I started walking again, it was toward home.

I was nearly there when I met the landlord. I couldn't stomach Smits and tried to sneak off, but it was too late. He had seen me.

"Samuel, how big you've got," he said, like he hadn't seen me in years, when we'd talked yesterday.

"Yes, sir," I said, remembering Ma's advice that there's no profit in being cheeky to landlords. I tried to edge past him, but he stepped in front of me.

"Ah, the legs," he groaned. "Up and down the stairs. Up and down. It's murder on the legs. And I've got three buildings to climb. Did you know that? Did you know I own three buildings? Of course you do."

I nodded.

"The legs go when you're old," he continued. "Don't get old, Samuel. It's a crime what God allows."

I didn't say anything. I knew that complaining about his legs wasn't the end of it.

"So, Samuel, how's your father?" he asked.

"The same," I replied, smashing my teeth together. There was more to come.

"Yes, of course. How sad. Ahh, life is cruel. It's a fact.

Your father has to accept it and get on," he said.

Life is cruel?

Not for him, it wasn't. Everybody knew his brother had brought him to America and set him up with three tenements. He was all clean clothes and a full belly, and he sure didn't know about sewing buttonholes for eight cents a hundred or burying a wife because of a fool son.

"Your father is behind with his rent," he said. "Must I suffer because of your father's misfortune? Is that fair?"

It wasn't the truth, about Pop being late with the rent. It was *me* who was late with the rent. Both me and him knew it. Knew that it was my work that mostly paid the rent, that I'd found the boarders to share the apartment and the expense. Why did he have to bother Pop?

"You're a resourceful boy, Samuel. I'm sure you must have something," he said.

The Liberty tickled my toes, but I plucked some pennies from my pocket and dropped them into his fist.

"That's all I got," I said.

He frowned. We both knew the coins didn't cover the rent.

"Tomorrow. I'll be back. Yes?" he said, smiling like a snake. He tried to pat my head, but I ducked and scooted away.

In the apartment, I saw that Fishblatt and the Taubs were gone. I guessed Fishblatt was knocking back beers at Brodie's, and the Taubs were out somewhere, enjoying an escape from the piles of fabric that awaited their sewing needles.

"Hey, Pop," I called as I entered and waved to him. He looked up from his work and nodded.

"Did ya eat?"

He shrugged his shoulders. I looked around for a dirty dish. Nothing.

"I'll be back in a minute, Pop," I said, and headed out again. I'd passed an apple man working his pushcart. Pop liked apples.

As I started for the door, Pop said, "Again, you're with the gangsters?"

"Whadaya talking about, Pop?" I asked, while I tried to figure out how he could possibly know about me and Monk.

"Again with the gangsters, the crazy boys from Jackson Street? Fishblatt saw you at Rutgers Square. He said there was problems. Crazy boys. Pickpockets. Again with the *meshugener gonefs*? Hasn't it brought enough sorrow?" Pop scolded.

"Nah, Pop," I began.

"You out all the time—"

"Working, Pop, I'm out—"

"Like before—"

"Pop—"

"With the Jackson Street gangsters—"

"Pop—"

"Your mother hated them. That's why she—"

"Pop!"

He glared at me.

"Me and Manny hawked papers and afterward went to Rutgers Square. We watched the dodge and the pickpockets at Rutgers but that's all!" I cried. "Geez, Pop. Fishblatt? The soused turd? Him ya listen to?"

Pop shrugged and went back to work.

After a few hours, I awoke. Everyone else was sleeping. Pop breathed heavily. I noticed he had slipped his own small pillow beneath my head as I slept. Careful not to wake him, I slid it back under his cheek. Then I sneaked out to Monk's.

"WHAT RATS THEY ARE!"

Everyone but Fink had arrived. I bent down and petted the cats while Monk talked with the others. Fink finally showed up, greeting the others with a big "Howyadoin'." Me, he sneered at.

We piled into a couple of horse-drawn cabs. Monk took me and Fink in one, and the others crammed into the other. Monk lit up a cigar and clouds of smoke filled the cab, a good thing, too, what with it covering Fink's stink of onion and rotten egg.

Crossing the Brooklyn Bridge was grand. Ships' lights dotted the bay like fireflies. One of them had to be the *Moravia*, I figured. Even Fink could see what a grand picture it was. He leaned far out of the cab to get a good view and then tried to spit down into the water, which seemed like a swell idea, so I leaned out too and gave it a try. But neither me nor Fink could get our spit to carry past the roadway.

"Get back into the cab before youse fall out," Monk growled, and we settled back into the seat.

In Brooklyn, we turned onto the wharf road. Monk took a salami out of his coat.

"Here ya go, ya little mutts," he muttered, sawing slices off with a pocketknife.

Fink pulled a smashed roll from his jacket. He was about to add his salami to it when Monk snatched it away.

"Give it here, ya dope," he growled, tearing off pieces for him and me before giving it back to Fink.

"A regular picnic, eh mutts?" Monk joked as he stuffed the food into his mouth.

Finally we stopped at a small brick warehouse with a sign that read PROUT BROS. CHANDLERS: ALL MANNER OF SHIPS' SUPPLIES. I could just make out a thin pier behind the building.

"Get out, mutts. We're there," Monk grunted. We hopped from the cab.

The horse-drawn cabs clip-clopped away, and everyone stretched legs and arms. Fink dug his fingers into his crotch and plucked at his clothes.

"Ya lose something?" Levy asked. Everybody laughed.

Fink glared and growled, "Yeah, sez you!"

It made no sense, but what do you expect from a chowderhead like Fink?

Monk pulled open a large double door in the front of the warehouse. He glanced into the shadows for a moment, then barked, "Prout, are ya there? Git out here."

But the only answer was the sound of the water lapping against the nearby bulkhead.

Monk plodded around the warehouse, muttering the most vile curses. After a moment, he marched over to Murphy and grabbed his ear and pulled, making him squeal.

"Well, wherz Prout, ya lousy creep? Ya said he'd be here!" Monk barked. Murphy gurgled something, but it was impossible to understand what he said, what with Monk twisting his ear something awful. The others smirked at Murphy's pain and seemed to enjoy the show. What rats they are, I thought.

Monk dragged Murphy toward the water.

"Murphy don't swim," Levy whispered.

Murphy whined, "*Don't, Monk!* It's not my fault that Prout isn't here, I told him—"

"Give it a rest, ya miserable croaking frog," called a voice from out of the gloom of the harbor.

"That you, Prout?" Monk yelled.

Like a ghost thickening into view, a boat and two men sailed up. On the front of the ship was painted THE LIMERICK MAID. Its sail dropped, slowing the boat as it came alongside the pier. One of the sailors scooped up a line from the boat, hopped neatly ashore, and tied the boat to a piling. It was like reining in a pony.

The sailor strode toward us and asked, "So, what's all the fuss?"

"Yer late!" Monk swore.

"Not late, just a wee bit tardy."

"Swallow it, Prout," Monk growled. "I paid ya to be here and I expect to get what I paid fer."

Prout's hard, leathery looks gave him the air of someone not to be trifled with. He slipped his thumbs behind the suspenders of his dirty canvas pants and said, "A boat don't sail on a by-the-minute schedule like the railroad. I said I'd be here around midnight, and it's about midnight now."

"Don't press yer luck," Monk warned.

He shrugged. I think there was little in the world that terrorized Prout.

We piled into the boat. It tipped and rocked, and I thought we were going to flip over. I found a bit of boat hardware to grasp.

The ship's sail went up and filled in a twinkling. The small boat leaped forward as Prout steered it toward the open bay.

The city and its lights fell behind us. Sometimes, something blacker than the night would loom out of the darkness and we'd brush past an anchored ship. It was like a monster leaping out of the dark. It scared me awful the first time it happened.

Spray came over the front of the boat, and it wasn't long before we were all damp and chilled. I was glad when Prout finally muttered, "Ahoy! Off the starboard bow. The *Moravia*."

Plain Stupid

Monk growled, "Get going, ya little rats. We don't have all night," sending Fink and me scampering to a rope ladder hanging from the steamship.

"Don't make a mess of it, ya slobs," said Tilson as we passed him.

"Soak yerself," Fink replied, and I grunted low in agreement.

Fink was first up the ladder, fumbling a bit. "Hurry up," I said, and he growled.

He climbed a few rungs, and I grabbed hold of the ladder. The thing was slimy and smelled like dead fish, and I fumbled like Fink had.

"Be quick," Monk whispered.

The *Limerick Maid* drifted away, leaving Fink and me hanging above the black water. Small waves slapped the *Moravia*'s hull. My gut clenched at the thought of falling. Going up that ladder was like climbing an ice pole. We slipped and slid.

Suddenly, Fink lost his grip and crashed onto my head and shoulders. I tightened my hands but the slimy rope ran through them and we fell. Then one of my feet went through a ladder rung, catching my leg and stopping us short. It felt like a saw against my leg, what with the weight of both Izzy and me bearing down on it. But I didn't scream out or nothing. I stayed quiet, just like Monk would have wanted me to.

Fink, on the other hand, was moaning, or some such sound.

"Shut up, ya idiot. Ya want somebody to hear us?" I whispered. I pushed him off of me and back up the ladder.

Instead of thanking me for saving us from a long fall into the dark water, Fink growled, "Stop shoving, ya Mick bastard."

It seemed like forever to reach the top. Fink stopped and craned his head about, making sure everything was clear. Then he slithered on deck and I followed. We pressed ourselves against the railing. On the deck opposite us was something like a long house that occupied the middle of the ship. I'm sure sailors have a special name for such a house, as they do for everything on a ship, but I didn't know it.

And it hit me, right then, that I was on a *cholera* ship. How would you stop yourself from getting cholera? I wondered. Should I take short breaths or try not to touch anything? I was plain stupid to think I could do either for very long. I finally figured the best thing to do was get the bird as quickly as we could and get off the damn boat!

"We can't stay here," I whispered to Fink, pushing him toward the front of the Moravia. I chased after and caught him at the base of a tall ventilation duct sprouting from the deck like a giant curved horn. Fink's breath raced and his eyes darted. I coulda sworn he was scared, but the thought of a frightened Izzy Fink was hard to swallow.

"Whadda we do now?" he croaked.

"Monk said the bird was in a lower hold," I said.

"Where the hell is that?" he asked.

"Where we are now, it's like the roof of a tenement. The bird's in the basement," I explained.

Scuttling off on my hands and knees, I got to a hatchway. It was quiet as death. I sneaked in and found myself in a dimly lit, narrow passageway.

"Come on," I whispered, and Fink trailed me. We stayed glued to the passageway wall. We listened to the *tap-tap* of the steps and then there was a grunt, metal squealing, and the loud *bang* of a hatch closing. My guts dropped like a cobblestone from a tenement roof.

A cold sweat I was in, and breathing heavy and frozen to the wall. It was the other voices that got me moving. I hardly heard them at first, them being faint and far off, like listening to a conversation through a wall. And that's what I thought, a couple of mugs talking in a far-off cabin. But then the voices got louder and closer. They were coming from a nearby cross-passageway.

"Move," I ordered Fink, and we darted away. At a turn in the passageway, I stopped at the corner to peek back. Two men—sailors?—headed toward me. I shoved Fink and we ran.

If this was the East Side, I'd know an alley to duck into or a rooftop escape, but I was rank stupid about steamships and it made me choke on my heart. I could hear the men behind us, hear them approach the passageway corner. Once they made the turn, they'd spot us and we'd be sunk.

I was thinking all of my luck had turned to horse shit, but then another hatchway appeared. I pushed Fink through it.

A giant chain was heaped there, the anchor chain, I guessed. We slunk down behind the pile. The cruddy links smelled like the rain barrels you'd find in alleys, the ones with drowned rats floating in the spunk water. I pressed my face close.

The men reached the hatch.

"Mother Mary, make them go, don't let them come in here," I prayed silently. "Please. I promise to do a *mitzvah* if you only make them go!"

They kept walking. Their steps became too faint to hear. I jumped up, grabbed Fink, and raced out the hatch and back down the passageway. Except for the scuffling we made as we ran, everything was silent. Another stairwell appeared, this one heading downward, and we took it. The steps were steeper than the earlier one, and it was more like a ladder than a stairs. We got to the bottom and I listened for a moment and we dashed off again.

We kept going through passageways and ladderways. I figured that as long as we was heading down into the guts of the ship, we was doing all right. And my blood was up, and running felt good.

Finally we reached a room filled with crates and boxes and barrels, some stacked to a high ceiling. This had to be the ship's hold, I said to myself, and was glad I didn't hear any disagreement in my head. I knelt beside a wooden crate and listened. The ship creaked and groaned something awful, but I didn't hear any voices.

"The damn bird has to be here somewhere," I whispered, and I started poking around for it.

Crates and boxes made tall piles. I climbed one to look around, but all I saw was more of the same. Fink ducked through a dark doorway, and I followed him into another large hold. There stood a large wire-enclosed box.

"*Da boid!*" Fink laughed.

The Duke of Prussia, perched inside a tall coop, was blinking at us through a metal screen covering the coop. The Duke seemed to be a fine pigeon, large and dark blue, but I don't know if my opinion of pigeons counted for much, in that the only ones I was familiar with were the ones crapping from the bridges and tenements and El tracks.

Fink busted the padlock on a side door with his boot and entered the coop.

"Don't scare him," I said, seeing the bird flapping its wings wildly as Fink's hands stabbed at it. Izzy grabbed the struggling bird from the crate.

"Careful!" I said.

Fink tucked the bird into his coat. I could see it squirming beneath the material. Fink made a face and said, "Yow! The damn thing is scatchin' and peckin' the hell outta me!"

The bird kept struggling until Fink flattened it with the palm of his hand, growling, "Give it a rest."

It squawked awful and stopped jumping underneath Fink's coat.

"Geez, Fink, you've squashed it to death!" I cried.

"Ya got holes in yer head, Glodsky. Can't ya see it still squirming?" he spat.

Fink was right. I could see the bird moving beneath his coat.

It began to squeak, and Fink said, "Sounds okay t'me." We scooted off, climbing the ladder out of the hold and up to the next deck.

Then the most awful groaning, low and rumbling, ran through the ship. It took me a moment to guess it was the *Moravia*'s engines come to life. A metallic clattering sound joined the boilers, and the awful, echoing noise almost deafened me.

"What the hell is that?" Fink asked.

"I think the engines have been started and the anchor is coming up. I think they're heading out."

"This thing can sail anywhere it wants, but not with me!" Fink grunted, and raced away. Not wanting to sail away with the *Moravia*, either, I stayed on his heels.

Doors along the hallway began swinging open and people spilled out and swallowed us in a crowd of shouting and crying men, women, and children. The *Moravia*'s panicked passengers made an awful racket. Words I'd never heard before flew past my ears. It took everything not to fall and be crushed by the crowd. Nobody gave me a second glance. The crowd swept me up one stairwell and then another, until we all spilled out onto the top deck. In the crush, I lost Fink.

I raced to the front of the ship and the rope ladder.

I looked down. There hung Fink at the bottom, one hand on the ladder, the other waving madly to the *Limerick Maid* as it glided toward him.

The *Moravia*'s whistle blew and the big ship shuddered as it began to steam off. I hopped the rail and clambered down the slick ladder.

"Monk, I got the bird!" Fink called.

The little sailboat nosed closer. I had made it halfway

down the ladder when Prout swerved beneath Fink and he dropped into the boat like a sack of potatoes.

"I got it, Monk! I got it!" Izzy shouted, reaching into his coat and removing the Duke. Monk scooped up the pigeon with both hands, and then pushed it into a small box. With that, the *Limerick Maid* slid away from the *Moravia*'s hull. The black water between the ship and the boat grew.

They were leaving me behind.

"Come back, Monk! I'm right here!" I yelled, scrambling down the ladder.

Monk and the others just stared at me as the distance between us lengthened.

"Come back!" I shouted.

A voice from above me shouted, "Hey, whadaya doin' down there?"

A sailor, bearded and red-faced, stared down at me from the rail.

"Git yer ass up here!" he ordered.

I slid farther away from him.

"Listen, ya slob, ya better git up here if ya know what's good fer ya!" he cried.

I climbed to lower rungs. Then my feet found air and I stopped. There was no farther to go.

"Crummy slob!" groaned the sailor as he started over the rail and down the ladder.

Then a hand grabbed the collar of my jacket and

yanked me off the ladder, slamming me onto the deck of the *Limerick Maid*.

Monk had come back for me.

"Let's beat it!" Monk said. The small boat glided away.

I glanced back at the *Moravia*. The angry sailor shook his fist at me; then he and the great ship were swallowed by the night.

"Thanks, Monk," I said, but he had already turned his back on me and was gazing through the screen box holding the Duke of Prussia.

"I woulda left ya hanging," Tilson, the Horse Poisoner, laughed. "Yer lucky Fink got back the bird and set Monk in a grand mood," he continued.

"Whadaya talking about? Him and me got the bird together," I argued.

The Poisoner chuckled and said, "Kid, only one of ya came off that boat with the bird and that was Fink. And that's the only thing that matters. Everything else is fairy tales and bunk now."

Me and Fink had shared the risks, but he'd won the glory, at least in Monk's eyes—and wasn't that the point?

The *Limerick Maid* sailed back to Brooklyn. No one spoke to me. Two cabs awaited us. Monk, the bird, and Izzy shared one, and me and the others crammed into the other. Levy and Murphy fell asleep. The Poisoner lit a stogie. Its stink fit my mood—I was foul with anger.

Dawn rose orange and pink over the Lower East Side as the cabs dropped us at Monk's pet store.

"Youse guys get some rest," Monk told the men, sending them on their way, leaving only Fink and me.

"Here ya go, kid," Monk said, and handed Fink a couple of fivers. Fink's eyes nearly popped out of his head at the sight.

Then Monk flipped a silver dollar to me.

"What gives, Monk? I done the job just like Fink. How come he gets ten bucks and I get one?" I asked.

"That's not how Fink tells it. Sez ya couldn't find yer arse with both hands, much less the boid.

"Soze the way I sees it, a little pisher like you should be lucky walking away with a buck in his pocket instead of a lump on his head. Beat it before I change my mind," he said, stepping over the cats loafing at the entrance, and disappeared through the door.

I looked at the coin in my palm. I shoulda thrown the coin after him and told him to soak himself. That's what I shoulda done, but I didn't. Maybe J. P. Morgan could throw away money, but I couldn't. I stuck the buck in my pocket and headed home. Needless to say, me and Fink didn't shake hands.

Fishblatt snored in a corner, as the Taub brothers sewed nearby. Pop sat at the table and sipped tea. He waved me over and I sat down beside him. After being up all night, you'd think I'd be tired, but I wasn't. Thinking about Monk and Fink had built a fire under me. I couldn't sit still. I drummed the table with my fingers.

"All night. Out?" Pop said.

I nodded. There was no point telling him I'd got skinned, so I lied. "Spent the night at Manny's."

Pop touched my sleeve and said, "Stand still."

Quickly threading a needle, he began darning a tear at the corner of my jacket pocket. When he finished, he patted the repair and murmured, "Good."

"Thanks, Pop," I said. He nodded, then returned his attention to the millionth buttonhole to be sewn.

I laid down my head on folded arms and closed my eyes. Thoughts of Monk, Fink, and the Duke lurched in my head. I heard Pop leave the table and return to work. Heard him lift the garments. Heard the gentle sweep of his hand as his needle went in and out. I slowly, slowly drifted to sleep.

FINK'S ONLY SOFT SPOT

You would have thought I'd sleep a hundred hours afterward. But what with the Taubs and Pop knocking around, making tea and gathering fabric, I awoke. Thoughts about the cholera ship began clattering around in my head like bolts in a bucket, making a racket that left me with nothing to do but get up and look for work.

Fiss, Doerr, and Carroll's already had three kids working when I got there. Hawking newspapers seemed like the only thing left, so I headed downtown, but the thought of selling papers without Manny made me drag my feet the whole way. When I got there, all the good corners were taken by other newsies. Not seeing the point of buying papers I wouldn't be able to unload, I trudged to the Battery. It was there that I found Duncy Napoli.

Duncy and some other kids were flying derbies across the sidewalk, spinning them back and forth like a game of catch. A grand time they were having, laughing and joking.

"Samuel!" Duncy cried when he noticed me, and clapped me on the shoulder. Then he launched into a story about getting a bunch of cheap derbies to skin the new immigrants with, only to find no greenies to buy them.

"I'm out three bucks if I can't sell these hats," Duncy moaned. But he kept smiling, which was a great thing about Duncy. He never seemed to get low. I wish I could be the same way.

"I saw that mug Fink before," he added. "He was wearing a new jacket and cap. Had his ma with him. Parading her down the Bowery, huge smile plastered on his face. They ducked into Kaplan's Clothes, and when they come out, Fink's ma is wearing a brand-new shawl. Last I saw them, they were stopping at Stein's fer a fancy lunch. I wonder who he robbed?"

Me.

"Can ya believe it? Isadore Fink and his mama?" Duncy laughed. "Okay, it isn't a surprise, him looking out fer his ma. Them two came to America together alone. No pop or other kids. Each other is all they got in the world."

I shrugged.

"I guess it's the only soft spot Fink's got. Mothers. Remember how he bawled when yer ma . . . well, the day at the waterfront?"

My eyes widened.

"Geez, Sam, ya must have heard about that?"

I shook my head.

"That day, right afterward, Fink swore to everyone that he'd never tossed a stone. Said he'd been on the stairwell pounding an Irish kid and never made it to the roof. Said he wasn't sure if a Yid or a Mick tossed the brick. Said it was an awful thing about yer ma. Then he ran off, crying. Later, he wouldn't let anyone talk about it, him being a tough guy and all."

"I don't believe it," I murmured.

"It's the truth, Sam. You know I got my ways of knowing stuff and, believe me, it's true. Cross my heart, hope to die," Duncy said.

A group of greenhorns arrived, eyeing Duncy's derbies.

"I smell money!" Duncy exclaimed, and ran off to do business.

I wandered off, my head bursting with what he'd told me.

A part of me had always wanted to believe Fink was the one, the one who'd tossed the stone that had hit my ma. I figured what with him being a mug and a lowlife, it had to be. But Duncy said no. Sorting it out made my head ache.

I wandered down to Park Row and looked for Manny, figuring he'd be there angling for a job. And I was right.

"Sam!" he cried. In a flash, he was beside me, telling me he'd gotten a job as an errand boy for the *Tribune*.

"And I bet pretty soon, I'll get a chance to be a copy

boy. After that, who knows, maybe a reporter!" he said, bursting with joy.

I slapped him on the back and told him it was the grandest news I'd heard in a long time, which was true. It would have been damn cruel to burden Manny with my low story.

"Let's go celebrate," I said, and we headed down Broadway.

We found a pushcart selling pretzels. I took the silver dollar Monk had given me from my coat and bought a couple of pretzels—round giant braided things the size of a dinner plate. They were still warm.

Manny tore into his like it was his first meal of the day, which it probably was. I was empty too, so him and me gnawed at the pretzels and didn't talk.

We both saw Fink and the Squab Wheelmen at the same time.

FINK'S FAT MOUTH

"Hey, half-a-Mick!" Fink called. I noticed he was wearing a new coat and boots. I guessed he wanted to crow some about his success with Monk. "How ya doing?"

He and the Squab Wheelmen drew up to us.

"I'm surprised yer still playing kiddy games with the Squabs, now that yer a big-time gangster friend of Monk's," I said.

Fink snickered. "It's killing ya, seeing me tight with Monk. He seen I got the brains and the nerve."

"Fink, yer mistaking *chutzpah* for brains. Ya stole the credit from me. Someday Monk's gonna catch up with yer lying. You'll see."

"Soak yerself, Glodsky. Ya thought ya could squeeze me out, but I skinned ya and it's chewing yer guts out."

Of course, Fink was right, it was eating me up inside. It was plain unfair, but who was I supposed to complain to? Instead, I said, "Yer just a slob, Fink, a lowlife, and someday yer gonna get yers."

Fink laughed, "Ain't gonna happen, half-a-Mick."

He was standing there, smiling all smuglike, when suddenly Manny shoved Fink into the Squab Wheelmen and sent them all tumbling.

With them in a screaming heap, Manny dragged me away.

We zigged and zagged through the sidewalk crowd. Tearing around a corner, we dodged people, horses, and wagons; darted across the street; and leaped to the sidewalk. Finally, Manny lifted his arm to stop.

"I don't know what come over me. Fink was puttin' on such grand airs and all, I couldn't swallow it anymore, so I let him have it!" Manny gasped with a grin.

"Geez, Manny, ya don't have to fight my battles for me, yer not my brother, ya know!" I barked.

"What's eating ya, Sam? When did clobbering Izzy Fink ever bother ya?" he asked.

That's when I told him the whole story about me, Fink, and Monk Eastman. He stayed glued to it until the end. Then he had a million questions, which I tried to answer. When I'd finished, Manny clapped me on the back and said my story was better than *Robin Hood*, the *Arabian Nights*, or any of the other stories we heard when we were still in school.

After glancing around for signs of Fink and the Squabs, we headed off. The street was thick with Wall Street gents, and we had to push our way through the packed crowd. At the Battery, we nuzzled up to a railing on the water. The harbor was jammed with boats. I stared out into the bay, hoping to catch a glimpse of the *Moravia*, knowing it was silly, what with the ship out of sight, who knows where. Still, I looked for it.

A ferry tied up near us and unloaded a dazed group of immigrants—new Americans!—stinking of whatever they got sprayed on them on Ellis Island to clean them up. I felt sorry for them as they stumbled from the ferry, eyes big, looking at their feet, hoping to see streets of gold. But all they saw was cobblestones and horse shit. They lurched ahead, dragging along everything they had in the world: suits and suitcases, bags and bundles. It was a flood, I tell ya, and there was no way to plug it up.

"Let's grab some lunch," I said.

We bought rye bread and herring to make sandwiches, and ate near the East River docks. Sails drooping in tied bundles from the masts of the giant sailboats reminded me of the clothes hung to dry from lines strung between tenements.

Manny told me how he'd landed the newspaper job, a long tale where God's Will and strokes of luck played central characters, all the while me knowing what had really happened was that Manny had made a pest of himself down at the *Tribune* and the only thing the editors could have done to end their torment was to hire Manny or kill him and, of course, killing him was out of the question.

I figured the newspaper people may not have known it yet, but they'd gotten a bargain treasure in Manny.

He finished the tale and said, "Of course, Sam, it means you and me won't be peddling papers together anymore."

I knew it wouldn't be half as swell hawking papers without Manny, but I kept that to myself and said, "Ferget it, kid. Maybe ya can get me a job at the *Trib*, too."

He laughed. I had as much chance of becoming a newspaperman as a Jew becoming mayor of New York.

Wandering, we ran into more greenhorns from Ellis Island. A bunch of them were trying on new derbies, laughing and clapping their hands. Why a simple derby was such a big deal was a mystery to me. I guessed it was some kind of measure of success. Them greenies loved the derbies. I swear they were throwing money at the kids who were selling them: Duncy and his pals.

Each of the four of them had a stack of derbies balanced on his head like a crazy, tall headdress. With every sale, their stacks of derbies got smaller. Duncy handled the money.

I tugged at Manny and said, "It's okay. I know the big guy."

He's a Dago and I'm a Yid and a Mick, but Duncy don't see it that way. "We all Americans," he once explained. He made friends with Yids, Micks, Coloreds, whatever.

Duncy explained how him and his friends had skinned the greenies, taking fifty cents for twenty-five-cent derbies.

"Them fools never caught on that they'd gotten their pants pulled down," Duncy joked. We all laughed.

Duncy looked hard at Manny and asked, "Ain't yer pop the singer? At yer church?"

"Yeah, he's the cantor, at the *shul*," Manny replied.

"That's like a singing rabbi, right?"

"Kinda."

"I heard him one time. I was outside the, uh, *shul*. Stayed glued there about twenty minutes listening, I liked it so much. Ya gonna be one of those cantors?"

"Naw. I'm starting work at the *Trib*. Gonna be a reporter, and . . ." Manny's voice trailed off. He gave me the heads-up with a nod. I turned to see that Fink and the Squabs were back.

Fink was moving fast and his fists were balled. There'd be no slipping a punch-up now, I thought. But as Fink got close, Duncy stepped between us. It brought Fink to a halt.

"I don't got no beef wid ya, Dago, so beat it," Fink said.

"I don't need a slob like you telling me to come and go," Duncy answered. Me, Manny, and Duncy's pals joined him.

"Soak yerself," Fink growled, turning slowly before walking away. I guess the odds weren't good enough for Izzy. As he left, he turned back and pointed a finger at me, his way of promising that this wasn't going to be the end of it.

"Thanks, Duncy," I said.

"Ferget it," he said. "Fink's a schmuck."

I offered to treat Duncy and his pals to pretzels, but he explained they had more derbies to pitch to the greenhorns. Manny and me walked home, our eyes out for Fink.

POISON COOKIE

"**N**umbskulls!" Fishblatt shouted at his bored students as I entered the apartment. He slapped a pale skinny kid on the side of the head and the others scuttled out of Fishblatt's reach. The lesson continued.

I picked up a newspaper lying in the corner but put it down right away. It made me think about Manny and his grand job with the *Tribune*. But it reminded me that my days of hawking newspapers with him were over. It just wouldn't be fun anymore, and where's the fun in a dodge if there's nobody there to share it with?

I was staring off into space, thinking of nothing but my own troubles, when I felt a nudge. It was Pop, holding out his teacup.

"Oh, sure, Pop. Right away," I said, and went to the kettle to heat water for him. "Hey, Pop, ya want to go over to Rutgers Square? We could grab something at a deli and have a picnic. Whadaya say?"

He shook his head, never looking up from his sewing. "Work," he muttered.

"Sure, Pop. I just thought . . . ," I said.

I made him a sweet tea 'cause he liked it that way, and placed the fresh cup next to him. When I turned to head out, I felt his hand around my wrist, stopping me.

"Thank you, Samuel," he said.

I nodded.

He returned to buttonholing, and I went to Moskowitz Umbrellas on Grand Street. It was a cockroach business that barely fed the Moskowitzes, but I'd made a few pennies helping out there before. Who knew, maybe there was something there today.

The dark shop smelled of sweat and glue. The three Moskowitz girls looked up from sewing umbrellas to glance at me, their fingers never missing a stitch. Mr. Moskowitz drilled holes in umbrella handles, a toothy grin stretching his face. Drilling holes was the best he could muster, having lost his mind right after leaving Ellis Island. America was just too much for him. The boss of the operation was Mrs. Moskowitz, a tiny woman with skin the color of old newspapers. She was steaming fabric onto the umbrellas' ribs.

"Whadaya want?" she asked.

"Do ya need any help? I've worked fer ya before," I said.

"I don't need help, I need rain!" she spat. "No rain, then no umbrella. No umbrella, then no money!

"Acch. Maybe basement needs cleaning. Stay. Work. A nickel. Yes?"

I cleaned the messy basement, stacking cloth, wood, and glue pots. When I'd finished, Mrs. Moskowitz gave the place a close going-over before handing me the five pennies.

I was setting out for Fiss, Doerr, and Carroll's when someone called, "Hey, kid! Glodsky!"

It was Tilson, the Horse Poisoner. He quick-stepped to me and asked, "Ya seen Fink? Monk's looking fer him."

"Last I saw him, he was downtown. Near the Battery. With the Squab Wheelmen. Why?" I said.

Yeah, for what? Does Monk need to give him another five bucks?

"Monk wants him, that's all," he said all smuglike, as if my job was to answer questions and not ask them. It made me like the Poisoner even less.

"Next time ya see him, tell him to get over to Monk's. Or else," he said.

"Fink's no friend of mine. What makes ya think I'll see him before you?" I said. I didn't want Tilson to get the idea that I was his messenger boy.

"If Monk wants Fink, ya'd be a smart kid to help him out," he replied with a nasty curl of his lip.

I was gonna tell him to soak himself when the most horrible racket exploded behind us, and I spun around. A streetcar and a dray wagon had crashed together. The dray's horse was on its side, flopping around like a fish out of water, screaming in awful high-pitched wails as it tried to right itself. Both its front legs were shattered and bone pushed through the skin of its forelegs. Blood sluiced out of the wounds.

It was Gunner, the horse that Bernie had looked so good atop the other day.

I didn't know much about horses, nothing more than what anybody could pick up from seeing them every day, but I knew the gelding's broken legs meant that poor Gunner was doomed.

"That horse should be shot. Where's the coppers when ya need them?" a nearby man muttered.

A crowd circled to watch Gunner cry and writhe. We all looked on stupidly at its agony. A couple of gutter-snipes picked up a stick and began poking the horse.

"Beat it, ya little slobs!" I barked, and chased them away.

Gunner tired, and his thrashing slowed.

"Where's the damn coppers?" I cried.

A dying horse ain't a novel attraction, so the crowd drifted away. When Tilson turned to leave, I grabbed his wrist and said, "Ya gotta put the horse outta its misery. Use yer poison."

"Ferget it. There's no charity jobs with me!" he said, pulling his wrist free of my hand.

"Wait!" I called. "What's it cost?"

"Huh?"

"To do a job. Ya know. To do a horse. What does it cost?"

"Ya ain't got it."

"What's it cost?"

The Poisoner gave me the once-over and said, "Fifteen bucks. Ya got that kind of money, big shot?"

I felt the coins in my pocket. With the money I'd earned hawking papers and at the Moskowitzes', and the Liberty Monk had given me, I had seven dollars. I pulled four from my pocket and pushed it into Tilson's palm.

"I ain't got fifteen, but here's four. That's four bucks ya won't have if ya just walk away. Poison the horse and walk away—it's the easiest money ya'll ever make," I said.

He pulled an oatmeal cookie from his coat and said, "Four bucks buys the cookie. You feed it to him."

He held the poison cookie up to my face and grinned. I snatched it away and Tilson left.

Gunner rocked weakly to and fro. His giant eyes bulged out as his hooves scraped at the cobblestones, making a sound like knives being sharpened. I slipped the cookie into my pocket and edged up on Gunner.

"It's okay, boy," I said, low and smooth. "It's okay."

His nostrils flared with each breath, and his sides rose and fell with every gasp of air.

"It's okay, boy," I repeated as I came up to his great head and stoked his muzzle.

I crushed the cookie into small bits and pushed them into Gunner's mouth. I grabbed the rein and held the horse steady, the whole time sweeping the poison into him.

"Hey! Ya hooligan! Whadaya doing?" yelled the drayman when he spotted me. He strode toward me. "Leave
the beast alone, ya slob!"

The last of the poison disappeared into the horse as the
drayman neared. I got to my feet and scurried away.

"Beat it, ya bum!" shouted the driver.

"Soak yerself!" I yelled.

Gunner lay flat. He lifted his head, moaned softly, and
dropped back to the ground. His chest heaved. His head
rose again and he turned toward me.

"It's okay, boy," I whispered.

Then he put his head onto the cobblestones and his
chest stopped heaving. His flank twitched. It twitched
again, and that was all.

A couple of kids walked up to him and yanked hairs
from his mane.

I stared at Gunner for a while. I remembered how fine
he and Bernie had looked as they paraded down Twenty-
fourth Street. Even a dead horse should be remembered
a bit before putting him out of your mind.

"Ya Messed Up
and Ya Gotta Pay!"

I turned away and tramped to Orchard Street, calculating that the hubbub of peddlers and shoppers there would yank my black thoughts away.

Pushcarts lined the sidewalk; the street was jammed with people. Business went on with shouts, cries, and barks. People haggled over pennies, and the sale of an egg was carried on like Queen Victoria's jewels changing hands.

I plunged into the crowd. I got pushed, shoved, and stepped on as I wormed through the shoppers. For a moment, I got trapped between a large gray-haired woman and a frog-eyed peddler arguing over a bad tomato.

I squeezed past them and came to an apple cart stacked high with bright fruit. I reached in my pocket for change to buy a couple, one for me and the other to bring back to Pop. Then I remembered spending it all on Tilson's cookie, and the memory of Gunner made me as black as when I had entered Orchard Street.

A hand grabbed my shoulder and spun me around.

Fink!

I quickly peeled his hand from my coat and backed away from the punch that I was sure would follow. But him and me were squashed together by the crowd and I couldn't get away. I cocked my fist, but Fink raised his open hands and cried, "Hold on!"

His eyes pleaded and his hands shook—not what I was expecting. I glanced around to see if it was some kind of a dodge so Fink's pals could jump me. But there were only shoppers and peddlers. Here I was, expecting a licking from Fink, and instead, he just stood there, looking like he was gonna cry.

"Ya gotta help me. Monk's after me. *Everybody's* after me," he blubbered.

"Whadaya talking about? Monk's after ya? He needs to unload another five bucks on ya?" I snapped.

"*No!* If they catch me, he's gonna kill me!"

"Fink, ya liar! Why would Monk want to kill ya, what with ya being his grand hero, getting his damn bird and all," I said. "Go soak yerself!"

"I'm not skinning ya, Glodsky. Monk is after me. He really wants to kill me!" he cried, holding me by my coat. "It's because of the damn bird. The day after me and you was on the cholera ship, I met Monk at Broome Street. 'I wanna show ya the apartment I fixed up for the boid,' he sez—"

"Apartment? Whadaya mean?" I interrupted.

"You heard me. An apartment. The bird was gonna get its own apartment. On the third floor. He had the windows screened and was gonna let the bird live there. That's sweet, huh, a whole apartment for one lousy pigeon?

"Monk takes the bird outta the box. He's strokin' and pettin' the thing like it's his baby, cooing at it and chirping at it. It was disgusting, how he carried on. Then he sez to the bird, 'There's yer new home,' and he kinda tosses it toward a perch at the end of the apartment. But the damn thing doesn't fly! It falls to the ground like a horse turd.

"We just stared at it. Finally it gets to its feet and starts hopping around, crazylike, and one of its wings is stuck out funnylike. Monk grabs the bird and pokes its wing. 'Broken,' he sez.

"I asked Monk what that meant, 'broken.' Monk just sez, 'Broken. The wing is broken.' Sez he noticed right off when he pulled the bird outta the box back on Broome Street, sez he kept the news close so he could share it *special* with me.

"I don't like the way he sez 'special', but don't let on.

"'How'd that happen?' I sez instead, and Monk looks at me real hard and sez, 'Ya broke it!'"

Fink's face was white and his eyes were big. He continued, "'It wasn't me,' I sez to Monk, but all he sez is that it was my fault. 'Didn't ya grab the boid and stuff him in yer jacket?'

"'Yeah,' I sez.

"'Well, that's how ya did it, ya little slob,' Monk sez. 'That's when ya broke its wing!'"

Fink stopped talking.

"Didn't I tell ya to be careful?" I said to Fink, remembering back to the hold in the *Moravia*.

He looked up at me and cried, "I didn't mean to hurt the damn bird. I just wanted to grab him and get off that miserable cholera ship!

"Anyways, Monk wouldn't listen to me and kept on saying the wing's broken and it's my fault. I sez, 'Ya gotta be able to fix the wing, right? People break their arms and they get fixed up, right?' But Monk just shook his head. 'Naw,' he sez, 'the boid's done fer.' Then he lifts the bird up to my face and *wrings the bird's neck!*"

"Wringed its neck? Ya mean, he just killed it, just like that?" I asked.

He nodded wildly. "Yeah, wrung its neck and tossed it to the floor like a dirty cigar. Then he sez, 'Kid, ya messed up and ya gotta pay.'"

"Whadaya mean, 'pay'?"

"Whadaya think? When I heard that, I bolted outta there."

The crowd on Orchard Street swirled around us.

"Ya sure he meant to kill ya?" I asked

"Ya shoulda seen him, Sam. He meant business!"

It seemed crazy, Monk killing Fink over a pigeon. But

Monk was a tough customer, and hadn't he already killed a guy over that bird?

"Ya gotta help me," Fink moaned. "Ya just gotta."

Sez you, ya miserable slob, I wanted to say. Soak yerself, I wanted to say.

"Damn ya, Fink. Let's get outta here," I said, tugging him away.

We shoved our way through the milling shoppers until we broke free of the crowd at the Bowery. As we crossed the street, someone yelled, "Hey, kid, get over here!"

It was Chief of Police Devery, waving his nightstick and heading straight at us.

"Hold it, ya street Arabs!"

You didn't have to be Isaac Newton to figure out Devery meant to grab Fink. Everyone knew he was no better than a mug, and grabbing Fink was the least he could do, what with Monk probably paying him more than the Police Department was. I guess it dawned on Fink, too, 'cause he started sprinting up the Bowery the same instant I did, the banging of Devery's nightstick on the sidewalk following us as we ran.

"What are we gonna do?" Fink gasped.

"What about yer buddies, can they help?" I asked.

"Have ya got a hole in yer head? Who the hell is gonna help me? The Squab Wheelmen? Them are as thick as ticks with Monk. The Hester Streeters? They'd probably sell me out fer two bits."

109

Grand pals ya got there, Fink, I thought.

"What makes you think *I* won't sell ya out?" I asked.

Devery and three coppers appeared, looking high and low. We dashed across the empty lots on Delancey Street until we reached a rough shack with a dented stovepipe stuck out its roof. It was, I knew, Duncy's hideaway. We dived past the ratty coat hung across the entrance and crashed into a bunch of fellas roasting potatoes over a small open fire.

"Hey!"

"What gives!"

"Get outta here!"

Fink fell half into the fire, then screamed as he rolled clear. I ended up beneath a big kid, who pinned my shoulders with his knees. He slipped one hand around my throat and screamed something in Italian. I figured it wasn't anything nice.

"Duncy," I croaked. "Duncy, I'm friends with Duncy!"

He just choked me tighter, enough to squeeze the life out of me. Finally someone knocked him off me. It was Duncy.

"Give it a rest!" he barked. Everyone stopped struggling.

"What gives, Sam?" he asked, finding me and Fink and his pals all in a pile something of a surprise to him.

It took him a while to sort everything out. I gave Duncy the straight deal about me, Fink, Monk, and the bird.

"Jeez, Sam, ya got yerself into a real helluva pickle!" Duncy said. "Monk has an army of eyes ready to spy on Fink—lowlives and on-the-take coppers. Getting him outta the Lower East Side is gonna be a tough nut to crack."

"Yeah," I replied. "But I think I got a dodge."

Monk's Million Eyes

Duncy's gang, me, and Fink slipped out of the shack and ran toward a nearby tenement. We'd taken only a few steps when Devery and some other coppers came charging through the traffic right after us.

"Beat it!" I yelled.

I got to the tenement's stoop and looked back. Devery was nearly on Fink.

"Damn ya, Fink," I growled, running back.

I crashed into Devery just as he grabbed Fink. The three of us tumbled into the other cops, who were close behind, sending them flying like tenpins. Me and Fink leaped up and got away before the cops found their feet. We raced into the tenement and up to the roof.

It was filled with people using it like a park and a playground. There was a pigeon coop and a wooden water tower. Laundry hung from lines strung between the coop and the tower.

Me, Fink, and Duncy went to the water tower, while

the others headed across the roofs of neighboring tenements. Duncy pushed aside a loose plank and led us
inside the tower. It was empty and smelled like wet socks,
but Devery would never guess we were inside.

Through a crack in a plank, I watched Duncy's pals
move from roof to roof, hopping the small walls that
separated the tenements and ducking around the people,
pigeon coops, chimneys, and hung laundry blocking
their way.

Devery and the cops arrived, huffing and puffing.

"There they go," one of the cops said, pointing to
Duncy's pals several rooftops away. "Toward Broadway!"

"Damn, we're gonna lose them," another cop said.

"The hell we are!" Devery replied. "After 'em!"

When they'd gone, we climbed out of the tower and
headed in the opposite direction, toward the river. From
building to building we went. When we couldn't get to a
neighboring roof because of an empty lot or such, we'd go
down to the street and wait for Duncy to give the place
the once-over before waving us on to the next tenement.
The whole time, we'd keep an eye over our shoulders, on
the lookout for cops and gangsters.

I felt safe in the tenements and on their roofs. The
mugs and lowlifes were in the joints or working dodges
on the street. Still, it was hard going. Fink moaned, "I
gotta rest."

He slid down on his ass. Duncy took deep breaths as

he bent over, resting his hands on his knees. I leaned against the side of a brick chimney.

Fink groaned, "Yer plan, it stinks. Why can't we ride the El outta here?"

"And how do ya plan to get to the El? Waltz down Second Avenue and hop on?" I snapped. "Monk's got his gang after ya, the coppers after ya, and every lowlife and mug on the take after ya.

"If ya wanna keep yer skin, we gotta keep to the plan and sneak to the river and outta the Lower East Side. And if that means traveling over every rooftop between here and the East River, well that's what we gotta do. That's the only way I figure we can get to Dr. Biggs. He's sure to help us."

We got going again, crossing one tenement rooftop after another until the tenements stopped. A wide vacant lot separated us from the next building.

"Hell," Fink moaned, and Duncy nodded.

My legs ached as we climbed down the stairs to street level, them being tired from all our racing about.

As we got lower, we heard shouts and curses, and the screams got awful loud as we neared the lobby. There, two men were hollering at each other. Nearby, a woman huddled beside furniture and boxes, five small kids clinging to her legs. The landlord was throwing the man and his family out of the building. Other tenants streamed into the lobby, adding their two cents to the fight.

Squeezing past the argument and onto the street, we found our way blocked by a large crowd. A mob swarmed a tall, silver-haired swell passing nickels out to everyone.

Big Tim Sullivan.

Big Tim liked to parade around the neighborhood and give out coins or food. "Help the hurting," he liked to boast, and I suppose it did, but I think it was less about charity and more about vote-buying.

There was no way around Big Tim and the crowd.

I led Fink and Duncy to a basement door at the back of the tenement, making a cloud of dust as we ran. We tore open the door, jumped down the steps, and dived into a black room. Duncy slammed the door shut, making a hollow clang that echoed in the dark.

"Ya think there are bats in here?" Fink asked.

"Shudup, ya idiot," I snapped. Whether bats lived in crummy tenement basements was something I didn't want to think about.

"Anything would be better than this!" he whined.

"Anything? How about Monk catching ya? Would that be better?" I replied.

I sat down. My ass touched the ground, and it got damp quick. Didn't make no sense getting up and trying a new spot. Wet ass was wet ass, and I'd just have to endure it.

Duncy cracked open the door and stared out.

"Jeez, would ya look at that?" he said.

Big Tim had been joined by Monk and Devery. The three of them had their heads pressed together in some kind of powwow. Monk lifted his arm and pointed up and down the street while Big Tim nodded and Devery stroked his walrus mustache.

Were they talking about me and Fink?

A quick look at Duncy and I could tell he had the same question in his head.

It was a hell of a fix. Big Tim Sullivan, Monk, and Devery a stone's throw away. Not to mention the coppers and gangsters who were probably hovering nearby. There was nothing to do but wait.

"Ya think Big Tim is a big deal, right?" Duncy finally said, trying, I guess, to get our minds on something else. "Well, he's nobody, compared to Boss Croker. He *runs* this city, just like Boss Tweed did. The Bosses are the real rulers of New York. The mayor, the politicians, the coppers, all of them are in the Boss's and Tammany Hall's pocket.

"I once met Judge Plunkitt, a fine Tammany man, and he told me—," Duncy droned.

"Can we give it a rest, Duncy? Okay?" I said. His lecturing made my head ache.

An hour passed before it was safe to come out. We sprinted to the next tenement, leaped up its stoop, and dashed to the roof. Traveling by rooftop was grand. The

next time we had to come down to street level, there was
no Big Tim around to make trouble.

We got close to the river around dusk.

It's harder to see at that hour, what with color slipping
from the world like water leaking from a broken bucket.
Nothing looked familiar. It wasn't until I caught sight of
the river that it dawned on me it was the Mick neighborhood where my ma had died.

I hadn't been back since that day.

We wormed our way along the river. Fewer people loi-
tered on the roofs, what with it being dark now. It was a
good thing, too, since we were in a Mick neighborhood
and Duncy and Fink didn't look Irish by a long shot. That
being so, it seemed to me it made no sense having Duncy
act as our lookout between buildings. I said as much to
the others, but Fink didn't go for it, saying Devery must
have spied me during our tussle and figured me and Fink
were connected.

"One of Monk's spies will spot ya and I'll be done fer,"
Fink argued.

We kept going from roof to roof, with occasional
sprints between buildings separated by empty lots or
street corners. On Cherry Street, Duncy said we were
passing where Boss Tweed'd been born.

Geez, Duncy, I said to myself, I don't give two shakes
where the old crook started life. How was knowing that
gonna help me now? Help me ever? I let my anger boil a

bit before I kicked myself for being so small. Wasn't
Duncy taking a hell of a risk for me?

Another vacant lot appeared ahead of us and we
started down the stairwell toward the street, making our
way through the crowded tenement hallways, Duncy's
and Fink's caps pulled low to avoid notice. Duncy left us
in the tenement as he checked the sidewalk. He glanced
up and down the street and was about to give us the okay
when three thick-shouldered Mick kids marched up to
him. The biggest one smacked Duncy's cap off while the
other two pinned his arms.

"What's a greasy Dago like you doing around here?"
growled the big kid, grabbing Duncy's jacket and pulling
him close.

"Let's beat it," Fink whispered, and turned to head
back to the roof.

"Wait a second," I hissed.

Duncy was in for a licking. The big Micks shoved him
around. When they stepped into the light of a street
lamp, I got a good look at them. The biggest one looked
familiar.

"Malachy!" I yelled, and ran from the tenement.

He spun around sharply. The sight of me must have
shocked him a bit, 'cause his grip on Duncy slipped, just
enough for Duncy to push back and swing his boot at
Malachy's nuts, which, as you'd expect, wasn't happily
received by Malachy. I dashed down the stoop and

wedged myself between Malachy and Duncy.

Malachy had grown since our last meeting. He'd sprung up and was a head taller than me, but it was his heft that surprised me. Where he once was wiry and thin, he was now thick and blocky, like a full-grown man.

Malachy, Duncy, me, and the other two Micks rocked back and forth for a bit, curses flying around like pigeons over bread crumbs. With him still gripping Duncy, I rushed through the story, and somewhere I may have let on that Fink was a friend of mine. Finally I was able to get them settled down to listen to me.

You might ask why I did that, and this is my answer. I was putting quite a bit on Malachy's plate as it was, showing up out of the blue and with Italian and Jewish kids, and forcing something of a compromise on Malachy by insisting he not thrash the Dago and Yid in question, so I decided to hold back on the part of the story about me and Fink really being enemies, my reasons for helping him not so clear even to me.

"Where's this kid, the Yid?" Malachy asked at the end of my tale.

I waved to Fink, who'd stayed hidden in the tenement entrance the whole time. He trudged down the stoop, slowly and nervously glancing about as he did.

I figured Malachy and Fink wouldn't recognize each other from the brawl last summer, guessing the wild action made the chances of them getting a good look at each other pretty long. And I was right: They didn't know each other from Adam.

Maybe because of my ma and all, but Malachy was grand about helping us. He led us to a beer-and-oysters joint after sending his pals home.

Fink's Hard Luck

Along the way, Malachy explained it wasn't him who'd thrown the cobblestones from the building that day. I guess he'd forgotten he already told me at Ma's funeral. He'd come right up to me then, and said he felt gawd-awful, that he was sorry, the whole time tears running down his cheeks.

Malachy ducked into the oyster joint right after collecting twenty-one cents from me, Duncy, and Fink. It was all we had. Duncy, me, and Fink pressed ourselves into the shadows and waited.

"How do we know the Mick didn't just skip out the back door with our money?" Fink asked.

"Because if he'd wanted our money, he and his pals woulda just taken it and thrown us in the East River afterward, that's how," I said.

Malachy strolled out with a bucket of beer in one hand and a bucket of oysters in the other, and led us to the docks. The edge of the pier was broken, and splintered planks poked over the river. Malachy scrambled down to the rocks below, careful not to spill the food.

"Come on, will ya? What are ya waiting for, a fancy invitation?" he said.

We climbed down and crept beneath the dock, it not being high enough for us to stand. The shore angled up and the space got narrower as we moved farther from the riverbank. Rocks, green with slime, filthy bits of rotten wood washed in from the river, mysterious rubbish of all sizes, and oyster shells were everywhere. It stunk, too, like the garbage from Grossman's Fish Market, except worse.

"Rest yer dogs, boys," Malachy said at a pile of thick wooden beams arranged around what looked like a fire pit. I figured this must be one of Malachy's gang's roosts.

"It ain't much, but we're safe here. The cops are too lazy to chase anyone under here," Malachy said.

He removed a knife from his pocket and forced open an oyster with it. He sucked it down with a noisy gulp. Then he sipped beer from the bucket.

It was oyster heaven after that, what with the four of us cracking open and swallowing oysters fast. We washed them down with beer.

Duncy said, "Ya really can't enjoy oysters without beer."

We grunted in agreement, me not mentioning not liking the stuff.

We jabbered as we ate, Duncy and Malachy learning

that they each had a sister named Mary and a brother named Joseph.

"Who'd a thunk it!" they laughed, causing such a ruckus I was sure we'd be found.

"I'm joining my brother Joe on the job someday," Malachy added. "He's a jailer on Blackwell's Island."

"So, yer getting a regular city job," I said.

"Ya bet. Like Joe says, 'Better to be paid per week than perhaps.'"

There was only the one bucket and four of us, so the oysters were gone damn fast. We finished the beer, Malachy taking the dregs. Afterward, we were all burps.

Duncy raised up and said, "Geez, I gotta piss."

He creeped back to the shore where he stood up and sprayed into the river. As he returned in a crouch, he banged his head against the dock planks. Rubbing the bruise, he said it was "worse than Sister Margaret's knuckles," making him and Malachy burst into belly laughs.

They got thick as ticks then, trading stories of nuns and priests who knocked them around during their earlier, brief appearance at church.

"Ya know, I was gonna be an altar boy," Duncy said.

"Ya don't say," Malachy replied.

"Yeah, but Sister Teresa drove me from it. She swatted my head like there was flies nesting there. And fer no reason!" Duncy exclaimed.

"Fer no reason, ya say," Malachy said.

Duncy went silent for a moment and then admitted, "Well, perhaps there was a bit of a reason."

"A *bit* of a reason, ya say." The two of them belly-laughed again.

"Wake the dead, why don't ya, laughing like that. *Meshugeners* I'm stuck with," Fink complained. "The damn racket yer making will bring every cop in the city."

Duncy and Malachy did their best to shut up, but laughter bubbled out of them like farts from a hansom-cab horse. Then Malachy asked, "How's yer pop, Sam?"

"The same. Not good," I answered.

"Sorry," he replied. "I'll pray to Saint Fillan fer him. He's the one to go to fer head problems."

"Whadaya talking about?" Fink said.

"Ya don't know about the saints?" Malachy asked.

"He's a Hebe. They ain't got saints," Duncy explained.

"Soze, whatsa saint?" Fink asked.

"Ya got a problem, ya pray to a special saint," Malachy said, but Fink just looked at him stupidly.

"Think of it this way, Fink," Duncy interrupted. "Let's say ya need a favor from Tammany Hall, like a job or a permit. But Boss Croker is too far up fer ya, outta reach, as it were. So what ya do is put the arm on somebody lower down, one of the ward captains, who'll take it up himself without bothering the boss. The saints got territories too, but not like the Tenth Ward or the Tenderloin, but taking care of kids or animals or people like Sam's pop, who ain't right in the head. They put in a good word with the Boss or get the job done theirselves."

Duncy said, "If ya need a saint, I'll pray to a good Italian saint like Bibiana or Raphael."

"Raphael's an archangel, ya slob, he ain't Italian!" Malachy growled.

"Yeah, well, Raphael sure ain't a dirty Mick's name!" Duncy replied.

"Dirty Mick!" Malachy cried, and started toward Duncy. I got between them quick.

"Have youse two mugs got holes in yer heads? Ya start a big enough ruckus down here and the cops are sure to find us. Geez, arguing over saints when neither of ya has been to church fer years. Give it a rest, will ya!" I said, and the two of them fell back on the beams.

"Saints. Idiots," Izzy muttered.

Duncy glared at him and said, "Well, there's a saint just fer you, Fink."

"Yeah, who?" he asked.

"Saint Magnus," Duncy said.

"What's his lookout?" Fink asked.

"Vermin," Duncy explained.

This time I joined Malachy and Duncy with their belly laughs.

"Slobs," Fink muttered, and crawled toward the river. He stood at its edge, unbuttoned his pants, and pissed.

And as he did, four hands reached down from the dock and lifted him out of sight with only a gurgle of surprise from Fink. It was like God Almighty had taken him away. I was pretty sure it was somebody almost as powerful, at least in the Lower East Side: Monk Eastman.

I just stood there, blinking at Fink's disappearance, until Malachy tore at my coat and hissed, "Cheese it!"

A racket erupted above us, shouting and boots scuffling the dock. Then I heard grunts and curses. A couple of cops had jumped off the dock, onto the riverbank.

"There they are!" one shouted.

"Over here," Malachy ordered. Me and Duncy followed him to where land sloped right up to the dock. There, Malachy stopped and stuck his head into the dirt!

What I hadn't seen right away was a small opening. He disappeared through it, and Duncy followed close behind. I glanced once more at the cops, still far behind, and squirmed through the hole and found myself tumbling into a coal bin. I swam around in the coal until Duncy and Malachy pulled me to my feet. Filthy we was, black from the coal dust, looking like players in a minstrel show.

"Quick!" Malachy said, and started shoveling rocks of coal toward the opening in the bin. Me and Duncy went right to work and covered the hole.

"Shhh," Malachy whispered, and we shut up.

Us being as quiet as the dead, we heard the cops

cursing as they searched for us. I figured they'd never find the hole. Hadn't I nearly missed it myself? Finally, the voices disappeared.

Malachy laughed, explaining how the hole connected the riverbank to a tenement coal bin, adding, "Me and the boys use the same getaway ferever and the cops never catch on!"

Then he led us out of the building to an alley, where we cleaned ourselves with water from a rain barrel. Afterward, Malachy dried his hand on his coat, stuck it out to shake, and said to me, "Best a'luck to ya, Sam. Sorry things didn't turn out the way ya wanted."

I stared at his hand and said, "Ya mean, that's it. Yer quitting? Yer not gonna help me find Fink?"

"Find Fink? Have ya lost yer senses?"

"It shouldn't be hard. The cops will deliver Fink to Monk, then—"

"Then what? Snatch the lousy mug from beneath Monk Eastman's nose? Do ya think maybe Monk and his gang might have something to say about that? I'd love to help ya, Sam, but I'm sorry, I want to live to my sixteenth birthday."

Duncy put his hand on my shoulder, and said, "Give it a rest, Sam. Ya done yer best fer Fink. Ya couldn't have done more fer the slob."

"And a slob he was," Malachy added. "It was plain to see. To tell ya the truth, I couldn't never figure why ya made a fuss over a lowlife like him. Why ya were helping him at all was a mystery."

Duncy said, "'Cause that's the way Sam is. He helped Fink because he *had* to."

I'm not sure what Duncy meant by that, but I'm pretty sure he meant it in a good way. Malachy just shrugged.

A FRENZY OF
FEATHERS AND SCREAMS

M e and Duncy headed off afterward, making sure there weren't any cops nearby. Without Fink, we didn't need to take as much care traveling, so we neared home quickly. Then Duncy and me split up, and I went home.

Outside the tenement, a mob of kids circled an organ grinder, an Italian man with a face like a squashed pumpkin. He played a hurdy-gurdy tune while his tiny monkey hopped and leaped through the crowd. It jumped on shoulders and heads, stopping here and there to tip its little fez hat and wait for a penny to be dropped in. Then off it would spring, back to the organ grinder, who would retrieve the coin. It was a grand show, and I laughed as hard as anyone else.

Suddenly, someone grabbed me from behind and threw me headlong into a hansom cab, where I skidded face-first on its floor.

"Move it," somebody growled, and the cab lurched forward. A boot clamped down on the back of my head.

"Don't move, ya slob," a voice ordered. It hurt awful, that boot, and I wasn't gonna do anything to make it worse.

The cab bounced over cobblestones for what seemed like forever before coming to a stop. I was pulled upward by my hair.

Devery!

"Come on, ya guttersnipe," he growled.

Him and a couple of other coppers dragged me out of the cab and into Monk Eastman's pet shop. Cats leaped out of the way and pigeons screamed. The small, bent man I'd met earlier climbed from his chair and met us.

"Where's Monk?" Devery asked.

"The roof. With the pigeons," answered the little man.

Devery grumbled, "Him and his damn birds."

"I bet ya don't have the courage to say that to his face," I said, not being able to keep myself from sassing him in return for the boot on my head.

"Shadup!" Devery snapped, slapping my head and throwing me to the floor. I scuttled away on my hands and knees, but Devery's pals grabbed me quick.

"Ya miserable *gonef!*" Devery hissed.

"I ain't no thief. And where'd ya pick up Yiddish, strong-arming the peddlers on Hester Street?" I argued.

"Ya lowlife Hebes are part of the job, lingo and all," he laughed.

"And what about Hebes from County Cork?" I asked.

"Whadaya talkin' about?" he replied.

"I'm the son of Kate Flynn, grandson of Daniel Megan Flynn of County Cork. That's what I'm talking about."

Devery, thick-head that he was, didn't know what to think, giving me hope that with a little luck, I could squeeze enough sympathy out of him to get out of whatever pickle I was in.

"Look at me, Devery, do I look like a Yid?" I asked.

He just stared at me.

"Are ya gonna let Monk get his hands on me?" I continued.

The questions were like monkey wrenches thrown into the slow-turning gears of Devery's mind. I figured one or two more and I could mess up his clockwork good. But a voice said, "Ah, ya got the little slob. Grand fer you, Devery."

Monk.

Towering over me, Monk pushed me hard, sending me stumbling to the floor.

My mind raced. Was there a dodge out of this?

"Here I wuz, thinking Fink had broken the bird"—*broken da boid*—"and it turns out, it was you."

What?

"Fink told me how ya tried to grab the Duke away from him and steal the glory. How ya probably broke da boid's wing."

Everything had got turned on its ear by Fink. Again.

131

"Ya shouldn't have done that," Monk said grimly.

My thoughts ran like sludge, and it took a while to catch Fink's dodge. He planned to save his own skin by pinning the pigeon's injury on me.

The miserable lowlife bastard!

"Ya shouldn't have done that," Monk repeated.

I coulda exploded, my anger was fever pitched. I'd gone out on a limb for Fink—and he'd sold me out.

"Ya numbskull! Ya rockhead! Skinned on the truth, ya miserable, flat-nosed, cauliflowered lowlife!" I shouted, fed up with the low deal I'd been getting.

Monk grabbed two great handfuls of my jacket and lifted me and then flung me through the air. My back slammed into the wire that penned the pigeons in the back of the room. It acted like a net, giving a little before springing me forward.

"Numbskull, am I!" Monk bellowed, and stomped toward me as I struggled to my feet. He grabbed again, lifting me with one hand as he cocked back the other into a meaty fist. Just as he was about to hit me, the little man said, "Monk, there's a guy outside, sez he's a doctor. Sez he's with the city. He wanted to come in, but I sez no. He said ya better come out then."

"Doctor? Whadaya mean, a doctor?" Monk growled.

The little man just shrugged his shoulders.

"Throw the little slob in wid the boids," Monk ordered, and he trudged outside. The little man unlocked the door to the pigeon coop, and Devery threw me in.

Feathers flew as the birds leaped and flew crazily away from me. The door was locked behind me, and I tried to find a place in the cramped space away from the wings that beat my head.

After a bit, the birds calmed down. A few wandered about, pecking at bits of bread scattered on the floor. Smack in the middle of the small gray birds stood Monk's giant pet pigeon. His head was cocked, his big-as-olives eyes giving me the once-over. I swear he looked down his beak at me the way some of the swells look down their nose at me. He flew to the floor, his big wings shooing away the other birds.

He ambled up to me, snapping up food along the way. The thought of him leaping up and flapping around my face made me press myself against the wall as he passed. I realized that there was a window right behind me, hidden behind paint the same color as the wall. A window was as good as a door out of the coop, I figured, and gave it a hard look. But then I remembered it faced the back of the building and the drop was all the way down to the basement. There was no going out that window without wings, unless I wanted a cracked head.

Monk's voice carried inside, and I heard curses and threats flying, the whole time thinking somebody was on the short side of a thrashing. But Monk kept at it, and I figured whoever was out there wasn't buying a word of it. Somebody was facing Monk down.

I couldn't hear the other man.

A doctor, the little guy had said. Then it hit me: Dr. Biggs!

I guessed he'd seen me snatched and had followed me back to Monk's. I shouted, "Dr. Biggs! Dr. Biggs!"

My yelling only frightened the pigeons, and they leaped into the air and made a racket of beating wings and piercing cries.

"Don't be frothing at the gob!" Devery warned, and banged the wire cage with his nightstick. "Or I'll be creasing yer head."

I backed away.

Monk stomped into the middle of the room. Then he shouted out to the door, "Do yer damnedest! Ya mean nothing to me, ya lousy slob!"

Devery and the others gave him space, like they was staying clear of a snapping dog.

"Who the hell does he think he is, talking to me like I'm some kinda everyday idiot. Sez he'll come in here if he wants! Public health, he sez. From the city, he sez! The city! Hell, on the Lower East Side, I *am* the city!"

"Who'd he say he was?" Devery asked.

"A doctor. Working for the city. Wanted in. Something about disease. Said he could quarantine the place if he wanted to. I sez not without Big Tim Sullivan's okay, he couldn't. The slob said he could do better than that. Like there's something bigger than Tammany Hall!"

"He left?" Devery asked.

Monk grunted yes, and then caught sight of me. Scowling, he said, "And you, ya fat-mouthed bum, I haven't forgotten about ya. So ya think I'm a rockhead, huh? Ya think I swallowed everything Fink told me. Well, I ain't got a hole in my head. I can smell a dodge a mile off. Fink says ya broke the Duke, but he's a lowlife liar. Ya say he did it.

"But I figure ya'd say anything to save yer skin, soze I can't tell which of youse guttersnipes are giving it to me straight. I figure the only thing to do is make both of ya pay the price and let the devil sort out the difference."

He loomed up to the wire cage, grabbing it with his hands and rattling it, grinning like a snake. The birds jumped into the air. I sprang back, but I was already at the wall and there was nowhere to go.

The birds calmed down. Monk's pet swooped down from its perch to his feet, cawing at him.

"Ya hungry, are ya?" Monk asked.

The bird hopped back and forth in front of me. Monk reached into his pocket and threw a heel of bread at the pigeon's feet.

The bird!

I went for the bread at the same instant as the bird did, grabbing it just as his beak took hold. For a moment, we played tug-of-war with the stale bread. While we did, I reached out and scooped him up. He flapped his wings madly and screamed awful as I tucked him up into my arms.

Monk jumped forward but bounced off the wire. The other birds went into a frenzy of feathers and screams.

"Let go of the bird!" Monk roared. *L'go ovda boid!*

"It's me or the damn bird!" I said.

"Ya hurt that bird and ya'll be finished!" Monk threatened.

"Ya already said I was finished. I just figured the pigeon would go first," I said, grabbing the bird's head with one of my hands. Monk yanked the coop door but the lock held.

"Let me go or I'll ring its neck," I hissed.

Monk looked at me through slit eyes. Then he turned to the little man and growled, "Let me in, Darby!"

Darby pulled a key from his vest. My back was to the painted window. I snapped my elbow back, shattering the glass. The noise scared the pigeons and they jumped into the air. As the birds swam in the air around me, I shooed them out the opening, freeing them to the sky.

"Ya bastard!" Monk howled, and raced toward me. I was sure he was going to plow right through the wire, so I lifted Monk's big pigeon and cocked my arm to twist its head off. Everybody froze.

"Open the damn door!" I growled.

Monk nodded, sending Darby scuttling toward the coop door. He fumbled with the key before unlocking it and backing away. The cops stood yards away, but Monk was anchored between me and the exit.

"Get outta my way, Monk," I demanded.

He didn't budge.

"Don't be an idiot. Not if ya want the bird back," I hissed.

He backed away. I started edging out of the coop. I kept my eyes on Monk and the cops.

I'd forgot completely about Darby. He jumped me near the door.

His arms came down around me, but they were thin arms, him being so small, and it was like getting grabbed by a kid. Still, he almost stripped me of the bird and I barely kept ahold of its feet. I elbowed myself free just as Monk bounded to me, arms outstretched. As he got close, I let go of the big pigeon, sending it flapping wildly in Monk's face. Arched back, he presented me with a grand target. So I kicked him in the nuts as hard as I could. He collapsed to the floor, howling.

I dashed out the door and leaped to the sidewalk, where I nearly crashed headlong into . . . Pop.

THE GRANDEST DODGE

This is how Manny explained it to me: He'd come by my apartment, hoping him and me could hawk papers one last time. He arrived in time to see me get snatched by Devery. Seeing me get hauled off in a hansom cab and not a police wagon, he figured it had something to do with Monk and that it probably stunk. He bolted upstairs and explained everything to Pop: Biggs, Monk, Fink, and the bird.

Manny wasn't sure what to expect from Pop, what with him in such a bad way for so long. But Manny said Pop jumped out of his chair, threw on his best jacket, and raced to Monk's, with Manny trailing behind. He tried to bust right in and snatch me but Monk's gangsters blocked the door. That's when he pulled the grandest dodge of all time.

"I'm Dr. Biggs of the New York City Health Department. I demand to enter and examine reports of cholera, of cholera, huh . . ."

"Within," Manny whispered from behind.

"*Within!*" Pop shouted. "I'm Dr. Biggs of the New York

138

City Health Department. I demand to enter and examine reports of cholera within!"

Pop figured, rightly as it turned out, that the odds were slim that they'd know who he really was and, being thick-skulled mugs, they'd be impressed with a big show of words.

"I demand to enter by order of the New York City Health Department!" he shouted again and again until Monk showed up.

Monk threatened all kinds of evil on Pop, but it was Monk who backed down and retreated into the pet store. Pop was figuring a new angle to get me out, when I came busting out.

Seeing him there shocked me, and I would have stayed frozen there, staring, if he hadn't given me a big hug and said, "Sammy, we better get out of here!"

But we didn't have to.

When Monk and his mugs raced out of the pet store after us, they ran into a crowd of reporters from the *World*, the *Journal*, the *Trib*, and the *Times*, them all there courtesy of Manny.

While Pop argued with Monk, Manny had raced off to nearby City Hall, where he knew there'd be a mob of reporters working the local beat. Manny said that a big battle was on between the Eastmans and the Hudson Dusters, a rival gang. The newsmen had scurried to Monk's and, finding him on the street, barraged him with questions about the upcoming fight. The whole scene was crazy, what with the reporters shouting and Monk screaming back that he didn't know what the hell they were talking about. Pop and I waltzed out of there like nobody's business.

Back home, we found Dr. Biggs. He'd come to hunt me down after not hearing from me for days, and had asked Miss Deitz where I lived.

After I unloaded my story on him, Biggs marched over to see a pal of his, the boss of the cops, another swell, named Roosevelt. Doc swore Teddy Roosevelt was honest, which was enough for me. Biggs told him the whole thing: about me, the bird, the cholera ship, Fink, and Monk Eastman. When Biggs was done, Roosevelt raced off with a squad of honest coppers and rescued Fink.

When the coppers brought him out of Broome Street, Fink was blubbering like a baby—at least that's what Manny was told by a *Trib* reporter who was there. I guess the notorious Izzy Fink was just a scared kid in the end.

Biggs later explained that Roosevelt couldn't arrest Monk, saying nobody was going to believe the word of a street kid, and besides, Monk had Tammany Hall friends who'd get him off the hook anyway. But Roosevelt warned Monk that if anything bad should happen to me, even the sniffles, Roosevelt would personally brain Monk.

Still, it was chancy, living on the Lower East Side afterward. Monk was something of a mad dog and just about impossible to reason with. Before stepping outside, I'd stick my nose out and give everything the once-over.

Now, not seeing Monk or any of his mugs, I bolted down the stoop steps and raced to the umbrella shop. Mr. Moskowitz's mind had entirely jumped its tracks, and he couldn't drill holes in umbrella handles anymore. I figured I could remind Mrs. Moskowitz what a grand job I'd done cleaning her basement, proof of what a good worker I was and right for the drilling job. But when I got there, I saw one of the daughters at the drill already, working the old man's job.

Seeing my future in the umbrella business disappear, I decided to head downtown instead and hawk papers. I bought a stack of newspapers from a new distributor, a Greek guy. He said his name was Taxos, and that he'd taken over from Hanratty.

"Did his thieving finally catch up with him?" I asked, but Taxos just shrugged as he hauled paper bundles from his wagon. It was a struggle, him being gray-haired and not strong-looking. Seeing him sweat so, I gave him a hand. We got the last of the papers to the sidewalk, and he slipped me a nickel, which was swell, what with me not asking for nothing.

I was heading off to hawk my papers, when he called, "Hey, kid! You come back tomorrow, early, and I'll pay you to help me for the day. Yes?"

"Sure!" I yelled, and tipped my hat.

Wasn't that grand, maybe a real job!

I hawked my papers, but the headline was something about President McKinley, nothing as exciting as cholera ships, and it was hard to get people to buy. I'm sure Manny could have invented a grand dodge of a headline, but I couldn't, and it seemed to take forever to sell the papers. I was finally down to my last few when a ruckus broke out behind me.

A kid on a bike had collided with a businessman. Angry shouts flew back and forth.

A Squab Wheelmen dodge.

The biker was a tall, skinny kid with rat eyes. Fink was nowhere to be seen.

I'd heard that living on the Lower East Side had become too much for Fink, what with Monk still itching to get him and no swell like Roosevelt on his side. He'd moved to the Bronx and found a job selling pickles.

Duncy said I shoulda given Fink a good beating. Made yer life a nightmare, he said. Nearly got ya killed, he said. He was right. Fink had made a mountain of troubles for me and deserved a punch or two. But that was how Monk and his mug friends would have handled it, and I'd seen enough of them rats to know I didn't want to be anything like them. Besides, I bet Fink's evil ways were sure to catch up with him someday, and he'd get the punishment he deserved.

Good riddance to him, I said to myself as I sold my last newspaper and headed home.

ME AND POP

O n the way, I ran into Manny. I was about to tell
him about Taxos and my future in the newspaper business, when he burst out, "Monk's
going to jail!"

He hopped around like he was on fire.

"Monk's going to jail. The Police Beat reporter told
me. Took a shot at a detective, the slob! The coppers have
already grabbed him and thrown him into Blackwell's
Island," Manny explained.

"Detective? Why?" I sputtered.

"Who knows? Maybe he just didn't like the mug's
face! Who cares? Monk's behind bars! And from what the
reporters at the paper said, he's gonna be there fer years.
The bigwigs at Tammany Hall aren't going to take his
side against the cops. The judges see their chance to get
him fer all the crimes he's slipped in the past. Ya see what
this means, Sam? Ya don't have to worry about Monk
bothering ya anymore! Ain't that grand?"

Manny and me started laughing and jumping and

clapping each other on the back. We stopped only to catch
our breath. In between gulps of air, I told him about Taxos,
and he slapped me on the shoulder in delight.

"I *knew* we'd be in the newspaper business together,"
he laughed.

He raced back to the newspaper soon after that, and I
headed off, too. On the way, I stopped for a bag of broken
cake.

I arrived home bursting.

I meant to rush to Pop, but I stopped short when I
smelled it. I don't know if a smell can be warm, but that's
what it seemed to me—warm and spicy and delicious. I
glanced at the stove and saw steaming pots. What gave?

Pop was lost in his sewing, and I had to tap him on
the shoulder. He looked up at me, smiled, and finished
the buttonhole. Then he put aside his work and walked
toward the cook pots. It was corned beef and cabbage.

Pop had cooked for me.

Grabbing a couple of plates, he ladled out heaps of it
for us. We had a swell lunch. I told him about Monk, and
having a job with the Greek guy. Pop clapped me on the
shoulder. When we finished, I remembered the broken
cake. Pop said we should have it outside, on the tenement stoop.

I had to squeeze next to him on the step to leave room
for people to pass. Pop divided the broken cake between
us and set the bag on the steps. We nibbled the sweets and

didn't talk, but that was okay, just sitting there was grand. Pop finished the crumbs. He closed his eyes, turned his face to the sun, and drew me closer.

I looked out on swarms of men in caps and derbies; women wearing shawls and thick, long skirts; horses pulling wagons and carts piled high with bolts of blue and green cloth, boxes of white china, crates of nails, ale barrels, paint buckets, wooden chairs, bricks, brushes, boots, bottles, buttons, and bloody sides of beef. Pushcarts jammed the sidewalk, and crowds of swaying shoppers pressed against them. Ragged kids weaved in and out of the throng, shouting, laughing, cursing, and stirring clouds of dust right up to the clothes flapping overhead from lines strung between buildings, waving like flags of brown, black, and white.

There were dodges and angles in that crazy parade, too, and I thought about newspapers to be hawked and pennies to be made.

Tomorrow.

What Is True and Real in This Book?

New York City became home to many of the millions flooding into America at the turn of the last century. Jews, Italians, Irish, Greeks, Turks, Slavs, among others, squashed themselves into teeming tenements, making Manhattan's Lower East Side the most densely populated place on the planet.

Competing for housing and jobs, and burdened with long-held prejudices and grievances, ethnic groups viewed each other across a no-man's-land of hostility and resentment. Kids adopted their parents' biases. Harpo Marx, of the Marx Brothers comedians, remembered his Jewish New York childhood and how he kept trinkets in his pockets, booty to be used to pay tribute to other, mostly Irish, kids for trespassing on their turf.

It wasn't always cultural or religious bias dividing people. Sometimes the ill feeling was parochial, and the mutual loathing of residents from neighboring villages in, say, Italy, continued in the New World. Race was less potent, mostly because New York, like most other

Northern cities, had a relatively small Black population until the massive population shift of people from the rural South to Northern factories in 1910.

For those readers unhappy with the coarse ethnic slurs mouthed by my characters, I have no apology to offer. *Yid, Dago, Mick*, and *street Arab* were freely used, reflecting the prejudicial stereotypes of the day. It is that world that I tried to describe in *The Notorious Izzy Fink*. In doing so, I employed slang and common expressions of that time for flavor and authenticity, drawing colloquialisms from contemporary literature. I employed *soak* as an all-around curse and epithet, although I can't say I am accurate. In 1899, the newsies seemed to use the word as a verb, as we might use *aggravate, prey on*, or *take advantage of*, as in, "A fella don't soak a lady."

In 1899, New York's *Journal* and *World* were struck by newsies, an event gleefully covered by un-struck competitors. The youngsters were quoted with their New Yawkese "dems," "dese," and "doz" intact, a patronizing practice resented by the kids. Still, the old newspaper articles offer a unique sampling of turn-of-the-century speech and jargon.

What, then, is true and real in this book?

Cholera ships did arrive in New York Harbor in 1892, but Monk Eastman was still just a teenager and years away from his gangsterdom.

Dr. Hermann Biggs was the Chief Inspector of the

Division of Pathology for the City of New York. He headed its bacteriological laboratories, the first of their kind for any municipality in the country. His history of the cholera outbreak of 1892 gives chillingly precise evidence of the reality of the threat. Biggs and other health officials were able to quarantine all the ships and spare the city a tragedy.

Jacob Riis was a crusading advocate for the poor, a newsman who learned to use a camera. The photographs in his best-known book, *How the Other Half Lives*, stirred the conscience of a nation. Still, reading Riis today, he strikes me as a tad smug. Perhaps it could be said of him that he loved humanity but disliked people.

Miss Deitz is an invented character, roughly inspired by Lillian Wald, founder of the Henry Street Settlement, a refuge for the poor of the Lower East Side.

Chief Devery was Police Chief of New York City, the last one, in fact. He was so corrupt that the state legislature abolished the office after him. Later, Devery and his cronies brought the Yankees baseball team to New York. (The Yankee logo of the intersecting *N* and *Y* was lifted from the police emblem.)

The Squab Wheelmen were a group of young pickpockets, a kind of junior auxiliary for the Eastman gang.

Monk Eastman was one of New York City's grand gangsters and lowlifes. Born Edward Osterman, he was a devout animal lover who owned a pet store before turning to the crime trade. He roamed the Lower East Side wearing a comically tiny bowler on his head and a pet pigeon perched on his shoulder. His other accessories included blackjacks, brass knuckles, and a club. He sent so many victims to the hospital emergency ward that ambulance drivers began calling it "Eastman's Pavilion." Things were going swimmingly for him until he was arrested for taking potshots at a Pinkerton detective and was thrown into Sing Sing Prison. Released ten years later, during the First World War, he enlisted and fought in France. His heroic exploits earned him the love and admiration of his fellow soldiers, who, at Monk's murder after the war—it seems he slipped back into the crime game—organized a grand funeral for him. Four thousand mourners showed up to say good-bye.

Of course, the grandest character in the book is New York City itself. Much of the old town has disappeared: The El—elevated train tracks—and Fiss, Doerr, and Carroll's Stable no longer exist. The McGurk's Suicide Hall building hung on for years and was just pulled down in 2005. Rutgers Square is now called Straus Square.

But the narrow streets are still there, frantic with immigrants, now Latinos and Asians. You don't have to close your eyes very tightly to imagine what it was like a hundred years ago. And if you wander the Lower East Side and stroll Rivington or Orchard Streets, rest on an

Eldridge Street stoop, or jump the sidewalk cracks on Forsyth, you can almost feel the heartbeat of everyone who has ever lived there.

Great cities are like that.